A
Long
Way
to
Whiskey
Creek

BY PATRICIA BEATTY

Blue Stars Watching
Bonanza Girl
Hail Columbia
Me, California Perkins
The Nickel-Plated Beauty
The Queen's Own Grove
The Sea Pair
Squaw Dog

PUBLISHED BY WILLIAM MORROW AND COMPANY

Indian Canoe-Maker

PUBLISHED BY THE CAXTON PRINTERS, LTD.

The Lady from Black Hawk

PUBLISHED BY MCGRAW-HILL BOOK COMPANY

BY JOHN AND PATRICIA BEATTY

The Royal Dirk
Witch Dog

PUBLISHED BY WILLIAM MORROW AND COMPANY

At the Seven Stars
Campion Towers
A Donkey for the King
Pirate Royal
The Queen's Wizard

PUBLISHED BY THE MACMILLAN COMPANY

A Long Way to Whiskey Creek

by Patricia Beatty

frontispiece
by Franz Altschuler

William Morrow & Company
New York

For
DOROTHY MCKENZIE
and
BETTY RYDER
of
Pasadena, California.

Contents

1
The
Despicable
Biped

Parker hauled on his best boots that morning, the pair with the Lone Star stitched into their top leathers. The last time he'd worn them was when Nerissa'd made Earl take him and the fryin'-size Quineys to the Baptist Church in Cottonwood. That church'd had the hardest benches on a skinny backside in the whole state of Texas.

As the boy tucked his trouser legs into the boot tops, he grinned, thinking of the day that lay before him. The bronc snapper was coming that morning. Parker sure hoped he'd take some notice of him this year, too.

There wasn't anybody he admired more than the rough-string rider. Still grinning, Parker strutted high-heeled across the rough floor of the bunkhouse, his wide hat on the back of his head. He jabbed his younger brother in the ribs and jerked the quilt off him.

"Git outa there, Leo. It's after sunup. The bronc snapper's comin' here from Tucker Springs today."

Leo lifted his head from the pillow and yawned. Quiney was written all over him, too. Parker's head was a dark-auburn, and Leo's was carrot color, but both were infested with cowlicks. Like his thirteen-year-old brother, Leo's face was so freckled it looked measled, and his round eyes were the same light blue.

Leo asked stupidly, "The bronc snapper?"

"Yep, to bust the two-year-olds. Earl said he was comin' last night, remember?"

"Now I do! Holy Snakes, Parker, I'm comin'." Leo staggered out of bed, leaving the quilt on the floor. But at Parker's warning headshake he picked it up and tucked it neatly into his bunk until it was as smooth as his brother's. Then he drew on his pants over his long underwear.

Parker grunted, looking at the neat bunk. "That'll set best with Nerissa," he said approvingly.

"Think Nerissa'll ever cotton to us Quineys?" asked the smaller boy.

Without replying, Parker led the way outside. For a time he stood breathing the cold April morning air while the barnyard hens scratched hopefully around

12

his boots. He looked at them in disgust. He didn't feed chickens. That was woman's work. Now he shaded his eyes with his hand to look to the east where the sun was humping itself higher over the limestone hills.

Nope, there wasn't any speck on the east road that led to Tucker Springs yet, so the bronc buster wasn't ridin' for the Quiney ranch. Parker looked down at a red rooster eyeing his boot and kicked it away before it could peck at his toes.

At last, he answered his brother's question. "Naw, I don' think old Nerissa ever will, Leo. She's had a whole six months to get used to us leppies that ain't got no ma or pa except out in our graveyard down by the creek. She ain't done it yet."

Parker went to the bench outside the kitchen where the wash basin, soap, and towel awaited. Between sputterings and splashings he went on talking, his head down. "When old Earl upped and married her in Fort Worth, he oughta told her about the five a us Quineys still here on the ranch. I heard tell the other day in Cottonwood Nerissa said to some ladies we Quineys was a 'rude awakenin' to a bride."

Parker felt Leo's hand tugging at his shirttail and became silent. He took the towel somebody handed him blindly and, burying his face in it, heard a clear high voice saying, "You were, indeed, a rude awakening to me, Parker, and not just the sight of you either, but everything else about your entire tribe!"

After he finished drying himself, his face gleaming

and his hair wet and dark, Parker murmured, embarrassed, "Mornin', ma'am." He looked up at Nerissa as Leo handed him the cowboy hat, and he jammed it back onto his head. Next Parker stared behind his brother's wife to where the three weaner gals, his sisters, stood lined up. All were redhaired, freckled, and unsmiling.

Nerissa, Parker had decided long ago, sure wasn't no handsome heifer. She was a skinny woman with pulled-back long dark braids, snapping blue eyes, and a sharp face, which was framed by a sunbonnet whenever she went out in the sun. She never wore anything on the ranch except plain blue calico, and white aprons. The only time the Quineys ever got to see her fancy duds and her bustle from Fort Worth was when she made them go to church.

"You get in to breakfast," she ordered all five children the moment after Leo had doused his head in the basin, too.

Parker went in last of all, careful not to brush against her. There at the top of the big table sat Earl, the oldest of the Quineys, his russet head bent over his fried eggs and beans. "Flannelmouth," Parker muttered under his breath. For sure Earl'd been a flannelmouth liar in Fort Worth to Nerissa. Livin' had been a sight better at the Quiney ranch when Earl had hired a Mexican woman from Cottonwood to look after the Quiney leppies. Yep, wearin' Nerissa's brand had took most of the hair right off Earl's hide. The way she ordered him around, nobody ever would have guessed

14

he'd fought Comanche Indians back in 1870, and that'd only been nine years ago!

Earl Quiney looked up and rumbled, "You git yer hat off, Parker. Men don' wear hats anymore to eat breakfast in this house. Mebbe yer the oldest one a the bunch still to home, but don' forgit you got yer manners to mind."

"Yes, sir." Parker took off his hat and put it on the chair next to him. Earl's big speckly fist could knock a man halfway to the Indian Territory. There wasn't any fryin'-size Quiney who hadn't learned that. Probably all of the other six Quiney leppies who'd growed up and gone away and got married or gone to work on somebody's cow ranch someplace else in Texas knew it, too.

Nerissa ought to be grateful all twelve Quineys hadn't been at home waitin' to greet Earl's bride. Parker picked up a dripping piece of bacon and chewed thoughtfully on it as he looked at Earl, who'd got roped and tied by a piece of calico. It was a lesson to him, all right, the way old Earl had changed! Bringin' Nerissa home had been a "rude awakenin' " to him and the weaner gals and Leo, too. Flannelmouth Earl hadn't told anybody about what he was goin' to do in Fort Worth—"gallin' " around when he was supposed to be buyin' some new horseflesh!

Although Earl Quiney ran some cows on his spread, he made his living from selling horses, tough, well-

15

broken ones. That's what the Quineys most prided themselves on. Before Earl had broken a leg four years back, he'd gentled his own stock for sale. Now, though, he hired the best bronc snapper in Santa Rosa County, the one cowboy Parker admired above all other men he knew.

Together he and Leo went out after breakfast toward the corral where the wild horses Parker and Earl had brought in from the range the day before waited. "I'm gonna be a rough-string rider, too," Parker announced as he watched the horses moving about nervously, switching their tails. Their ears flicked back as the boys stood with their arms hooked over the corral rail.

"I like the pinto," confided Leo, pointing to a small horse with white, black, and brown markings and a long black tail.

Parker spat into the dust. "How many times I got to tell ya, Leo, a pinto ain't worth much. Ain't ya never heard Earl say a pinto's a emotional horse? Git yourself a bay or chestnut." Parker swung himself up to straddle the top rail of the corral. From his "opry seat" he looked hopefully to the east again. No one was coming down that road. Then as Leo went to sit down at the foot of the big pecan tree that shaded the side of the barn, Parker stared west for a change toward Cottonwood.

"Leo, there's a rider comin'."

Leo got up at once. "Is it the bronc buster?"

Parker spat again and said disgustedly, "Naw, he's

16

comin' from the wrong way, but mebbe he's comin' here at that. Let's go up on the porch and wait."

The boys watched as the figure grew larger and larger, finally resolving into a long-haired, dark-faced stranger on a dun mare.

The rider reined in and spoke to the boys. "Howdy. Is this here the Quiney place?"

Parker stared at the brand on the mare's flank, not recognizing it. He answered, "Yes, sir."

"I got me a letter from Ruination up north a here for a Earl Quiney," said the stranger. "A man give it to me in Buffalo Notch to give to a Earl Quiney somewhere's near Cottonwood in Santa Rosa County."

"He's our brother. I'll give it to him. I'm Parker Quiney."

"Much obliged to ya." The stranger grunted, fished a letter out of his shirt pocket, handed it down, wheeled the mare about, and started west again.

"Much obliged to you!" Parker shouted after him. Then he examined the letter. The paper was tobacco-stained and tattered. "Looks like it's come a long ways," he told Leo. "You keep a lookout for the horse buster while I take this to Earl."

Parker found his brother and his wife still at the table, Nerissa with pencil and paper in front of her, adding a column of numbers as Earl scratched his head, reciting them from memory.

"Who was that ridin' in jest now, the bronc snapper?" asked Earl, sounding irritable.

17

"Nope, it wasn' anybody I ever set eyes on before. He brung you this." Parker gave the ragged letter to his brother, who looked at it, shook his head, and handed it to Nerissa.

Parker heard her sigh of exasperation as she opened the filthy envelope, then her gasp. "Oh, Earl, it's about your brother, Jesse!"

"What about Jess?"

"He's dead. The letter says he was shot and killed by another cowboy last January up in a line camp!"

Earl's big face grew sad. "Jess wasn' more'n twenty-one. Who shot him, Nerissa?"

"A man named Peterson—Starr Peterson. They had a gun fight and killed each other."

"I don' know him," said Earl Quiney dully. "Does it say what they was fightin' about?"

Nerissa shook her head. "The letter doesn't say."

"Who wrote it, gal?"

"A Mr. O'Hearne, the foreman of the ranch Jesse was working on. He says he and some of his cowboys buried Jesse and this Starr Peterson."

"Where's Jesse buried?" Earl asked, his eyes filling with tears. Parker never had seen him cry before.

"Mr. O'Hearne says on the banks of Whiskey Creek, near to Ruination." She put down the letter, sighing.

Earl reached for it and stared down at it. "I wish to God I coulda read it myself, Nerissa. It don' seem right at times like this that us Quineys ain't never had no schoolin'." He slowly folded the paper and put it into

18

his pocket. "Nerissa," he told her hoarsely, "you write the rest of us Quineys that ain't here and tell 'em. When we bring Jess back home to our graveyard, we'll have that preacher a yours out from Cottonwood and have him send Jess off right."

Nerissa, Parker thought, was surely surprised. "Earl, you told me once that Jesse told you he was going up to north Texas to look for work. That's hundreds of miles from here. Where is this Ruination?"

"I heard of it once," said Earl Quiney. "It's up near Indian Territory. That's near four hundred miles, I guess."

"But who'll go all that way after Jesse?" she asked.

Earl looked up at Parker, his gaze heavy. "I can't do it. I got horses and mules to bust and sell here. The oldest one at home'll have to go. That's the Quiney way. That'd be you, Parker. Hitch up the wagon, rope a mule, and trade it fer a coffin at the undertaker's in Cottonwood. Git a good one. While yer hitchin' up Hooraw and Pilgrim, Nerissa and the gals'll git ready the supplies you'll be needin'. Yer startin' fer Ruination and Whiskey Creek today."

Parker nodded calmly. "Can Leo come along?"

"*No!*" exploded Nerissa, standing up, her face awry with anger. "This is a terrible thing, Earl, sending a boy Parker's age four hundred miles—but not Leo, too. He's only nine years old!"

"All right, Nerissa, gal. Leo'll stay here."

"Then I got to go alone?" asked Parker.

19

"Looks that way, don' it? Unless you can find somebody who'll be willin' to go with ya," came from Earl.

Parker nodded and left the kitchen, with Nerissa arguing. There wasn' going to be any changin' of Earl's mind—no matter how long Nerissa talked this time. She wasn' going to dent Earl's thinkin' here. Quineys belonged in the Quiney graveyard, no place else.

As he started for the barn to harness and bring out the team, J.E.B. Stuart, Earl's dog, came running toward him, his tongue flapping. Parker scratched his ears and spoke softly to the black-and-white animal. "You been out all night chasin' jackrabbits, I bet, J.E.B. How'd ya like to go on up to Whiskey Creek with me?"

The dog at his side, Parker went by Leo, lolling under the pecan tree. Parker's thoughts were on his brother, Jesse. He didn't recollect him well at all. Jesse was the third oldest Quiney. He'd left home when Parker had been some smaller than Leo and never come back. About all he remembered about Jess was that he'd played the mouth organ real good and wore a silver ring shaped like a saddle. He'd traded a Mexican somethin' for it.

Leo came running behind him as Parker opened the barn door. "Where you goin', Parker? What was in the letter?"

"Jesse's got himself killed up north a ways," the older boy explained shortly. "I'm goin' there to fetch him back."

"Me, too?" asked Leo.

20

The Despicable Biped

"Naw, old Nerissa put a stop to that. You ain't big enough. She don' think I'm big enough neither, but Earl's sendin' me. I'm gonna miss the bronc snapper's bein' here. I wanted him to see I got myself boots jes' like his."

Leo's eyes filled with tears. "You're goin' alone, Parker?"

"No, I ain't goin' alone—not if I don' have to. I'll be wantin' enough food for two. I'll tell that to one a the weaner gals. Now don' you bawl. Quineys don't do that. Besides, I don't think you recollect Jesse at all, do ya?"

Parker didn't wait for a reply. He went into the barn, but his voice drifted back from the hay-smelling blackness. "Leo, git me a mule, the oldest one outa the bunch south a here. Git me that ten-dollar one that give us all the trouble last month."

Three hours later Parker Quiney, a rangy brown mule in tow, came into Cottonwood driving the Quiney wagon. Nodding to men on the tree-shaded street and tipping his hat to the ladies, he drove the chestnut and the white geldings to the undertaker's little shop in the center of town. While the team waited at the hitching post with J.E.B. Stuart, Parker did his business with the undertaker. He talked briefly to the man, then untied the mule from the wagon, and led it to the corral behind the shop, where he tied it as far as possible from a solitary steer.

21

Pointing to the steer, Parker asked, "Who else's gone and died?"

The man answered, "A little gal married to a rancher north a town. Mebbe you'd recollect her? She used to live at the Widow Bybee's a while back." The undertaker sighed. "Her husband paid me with that steer. Nobody in Texas ever's got much cash money since the war—only animal critters. I say the Yankees got all the money."

Parker nodded. That was true, all right. Earl traded horses for things a lot of the time. "How about a buryin' box for me?" he asked.

"You help me fetch it outside. It's over there."

Parker examined the plain wooden coffin carefully for bad workmanship. "It's got to be a good one," said the boy.

"You won't find no knotholes in it. I made it myself," boasted the man. He added, "You told me inside you was going near all the way to Indian territory. That's a long way north a here. Sorta young, ain't you, for that kinda thing?"

"I'm the oldest Quiney there is at home, mister. This here coffin'll do, I reckon."

Together they shoved the box into the back of the wagon next to some sacks of supplies. The man looked under the seat of the wagon and asked, "You got *two* Winchesters here, boy. Who else's goin'?"

Parker untied the team and hauled himself up onto the wagon seat. From there he said, "You gave me a

22

idea who, mister! Do you know if that fat yellow-headed kid's still livin' at the Widow Bybee's?

"I seen him only a half hour ago, traipsin' along behind her." The undertaker asked, "You know the Graber boy?"

"We was baptized last month in the river at the same meetin'. The water was colder'n the devil, and the preacher danged near drowned the both a us. I talked to the fat kid a couple times since then when the widow wasn' lookin'. I kinda took to him even if he does talk queer. Where'd you say you saw him today?"

"Carryin' a basket followin' the widow into the Mercantile Emporium."

"Much obliged to ya, mister." Expertly Parker swung the wagon around to go back the way he'd come. Then over his shoulder he called, "Watch out fer that mule I brung ya. He tried to kill a stallion in our corral last month and darned near done the job."

Parker laughed when he heard the undertaker's furious shouting and saw him shaking his fist. "You think you're a high-goin' whizzer, don't ya? Well, you ain't. You're jest a button, ya hear me. Don' you never come here to me again. Rattle yer hocks outa town to Indian country, and don' ya never come back!"

Waiting, Parker sat high on the wagon seat in front of the Mercantile Emporium. He tipped his hat to passing ladies again, and to a friend of Earl's who spied the coffin he explained what had happened up on Whiskey

Creek. This man was the only person who asked, though many folks saw the buryin' box. Quineys minded their own affairs. Cottonwood knew that. Moreover, Parker seldom took his eyes from the door of the Emporium.

At last it opened, and he leaned forward. A tall sour-faced woman wearing a black dress, shawl, and bonnet came striding out. Once on the street she snapped, "Come on, you despicable biped, and shut the door behind you so you don't let more flies in!"

Parker smiled as a short plump boy with long curling golden hair and a round pale face came out of the store. Parker Quiney took a quick inventory and shook his head. Jonathan Graber was a real sight. He wore heavy shoes with metal toes, ribbed stockings, knee pants, a coat, a white shirt, and a flopping blue tie around his neck. His hat was round with long ribbons on it. Carrying a basket over each arm, he looked purely miserable. There were vegetables sticking out of one of them, calico and yellow and red ribbons in the other. Parker watched him run after the Widow Bybee, who could outwalk half the men in town.

"Poor cuss," Parker said to J.E.B. Stuart, who was snoring now in the back of the wagon, tuckered out after his night of rabbit chasing. Parker thought of what he'd heard of the widow, who took in orphans the Santa Rosa County judge assigned to her. He'd heard tell, even if she never missed a Sunday in church, she was mean enough to kick a hog to death without her boots on. He wondered how in the name of all git out

24

the Graber kid stayed fat like that? Folks said the widow set a mighty poor table. Even worse, she was good friends with the Cottonwood wisdom bringer, the schoolmarm.

Parker pondered about the yellow-haired boy some more. He hadn't liked gettin' baptized neither in that freezin' water. Oh, he hadn' said much, but he'd had a look on his face that showed what he was thinkin', and he'd agreed when Parker'd muttered that it'd be a lot easier to get religion in the summer than in March! Graber had looked mad, too—as mad at the widow for makin' him go out in the creek as Parker'd been at old Nerissa.

When the widow and boy were out of sight, Parker got down from the wagon seat. He knew the man who owned the Emporium well enough to ask him questions without getting him riled up. Parker found him counting sacks of sugar and waited, sitting on a barrel, until he was finished. Then he asked, "What's a 'despicable biped'?"

The storekeeper laughed. "You musta heard the widow talkin'. She read them words once in a book, she says. I asked her what they meant. A biped's a person, you know, that's got only two feet. The other word means somethin' that makes a man want to hold his nose to keep from smellin' somethin' bad."

Parker asked, "You know anythin' about this here Graber she's got her hooks inta now?"

The man shook his head. "Not much, Parker. He's

25

sort of new to town. I heard that his pa went silver minin' to Old Mexico and hasn't come back. Folks think he's dead like his ma."

"Is he from hereabouts?"

"Mebbe. I dunno. He don' look it, does he?"

"He sure don'. He don' look to me like he ever seen a horse." Parker got up and stretched.

"Anythin' I can git for ya or Earl or the new Missus Quiney?" asked the storekeeper.

"Naw. Earl'll mos' likely be in pretty soon—when he gits our horses broke and sells 'em."

The man nodded. "You still got your heart set on bein' a rough-string rider, Parker?"

"Nothin' else'd suit me." He added, "Much obliged to ya," and left.

His mind was made up. There was going to be a three-quarter moon that night. That ought to be plenty of light.

Parker stayed in Cottonwood all that day at the far edge of town under some pecan trees. He ate the cornbread and bacon Nerissa'd given him, slept under the wagon most of the afternoon, had more cornbread after dark, then shivering, put on his heavy jacket to wait for the moonrise.

When he saw it, lopsided and white, through the spring leaves, he got up into the wagon again and sent Hooraw and Pilgrim walking slowly back through the

26

The Despicable Biped

town. "You keep shut up," he warned J.E.B. Stuart, padding beside the wagon.

The Widow Bybee's place was a two-story wood house, built as far as possible from the saloons and as close as possible to the church and school, it seemed to Parker. That was just like her, he reflected, to be where it was most quiet. He could use some saloon piano music now to cover up whatever noise he might make.

Leaving the team tied to a tree, Parker circled the house warily. There were a couple of lights from kerosene lanterns downstairs, but upstairs there was only one. And there was a tree outside that one window! That was good! The boy peeked into the parlor. Yep, there sat the widow with three half-growed gals. They were sewin', and she was readin' out loud out of a big book. There wasn' any boy there Parker could see. He reckoned Graber'd been sent up to bed early.

High-heeled boots weren't worth a hoot climbing a tree. Parker pulled his off and left them at its foot. Then he jumped high for a branch, caught it, swung back and forth for momentum, and hauled himself up into the tree.

One limb almost touched the upstairs window. Parker inched along it on his belly and called softly, "Graber. Hey, Graber!"

"Huh? Who's out there?" came a startled-sounding reply.

"Come here and see," hissed Parker Quiney.

In a moment the Graber boy's head was at the window, pushing it open wider. "Who's out there?"

Parker thought he sounded scared. "It's me, Parker Quiney. We got baptized together. I talked to ya a couple times since, remember?"

Now the yellow curls came out all the way. "I saw you today outside the Mercantile Emporium, too, didn't I?"

"Yup, you did." Parker came straight to the point. "How'd you like to run away from the widow tonight?"

"Huh?"

"Sure, run away. You don' like livin' here, do ya?"

Parker politely gave the other boy time to think and changed the subject. "What do folks call ya besides Jonathan?"

"What should they call me?"

"Anythin' but Jonathan. How about John or Nate? Take yer pick."

There was a long silence. "Nate, I guess. My father's named John." Then the Graber boy asked sharply, "What'll I call you? Parker sounds pretty funny to me!"

"I don' care. It was my ma's maiden name. I ain't got a middle one. Now how 'bout goin' away with me tonight?"

"Why ask *me?* Where to?" Nate was mighty suspicious.

Parker answered the last question first. "My brother Earl's sendin' me on a errand. I picked ya 'cause yer

28

the only other leppie I know my age. Ya didn't like bein' baptized either, and you hate the Widow Bybee. I took to ya, I guess. I'm gettin' shed for a while of a pesky woman, too, my brother's wife. I reckoned I oughta help ya out, seeing as how we had so much in common. I'm on my way north to Whiskey Creek." He paused for breath. "If my ma was alive, she'd never make me carry baskets and dress up like a porch-perchin' dude or call me a 'dispectful biped' like the widow does you."

" 'Despicable,' " corrected Nate. There was another long silence. Then he said, "All right, that 'despicable' decided it. I'm coming with you, Parker. Have you got anything to eat? I didn't have any supper tonight. That's the second time this week she's starved me!"

"Why didn' ya, Nate?"

"Because I didn't cross the street like she did to avoid passing a saloon door. I'll get ready to leave now."

From the tree limb Parker watched the other boy as he went back into the room. Holy Gatlins, Nate was wearing a nightshirt to sleep in instead of his underwear. "Come back here," he called once more. When Nate came, he whispered, "Don't bring that purty white thing on ya along."

"What should I bring, Parker?"

"We got quite a piece to travel even if I got a wagon to carry our stuff. Bring what's the warmest. I'll git on down and you can throw stuff to me. I'll catch it."

Without waiting for a reply, Parker went down the

tree, hauled on his boots, and checked to see that the widow was still reading. He took up a position below the upstairs window. First to rain down on his head was a cloth bundle—clothing, he imagined. He'd barely caught that and put it on the grass when the sodbuster shoes Nate'd been wearing came hurtling down and nearly brained him. Then came a large soft mass Parker reckoned to be Nate's bedclothing, to be used as a bedroll. Last of all floated down the round beribboned hat he'd also seen that day. Parker grabbed it in midair and shoved it behind one of the widow's bushes. Maybe he'd have to go to Whiskey Creek with somebody wearin' sodbuster shoes and yellow curls—but not with a hat like that one.

Puffing, Nate Graber finally shinnied down. Parker looked at him and said not a word. The knee britches were still there and so was the white shirt, but the tie, coat, and stiff collar were gone. Nate wore a heavy jacket some sizes too big for him. "It was my father's," he explained proudly.

"Get yer shoes and come on," ordered Parker.

Their arms laden with Graber belongings, the boys crept behind the house to where the wagon and team stood in blackness under the trees.

"Pitch yer stuff in back," said Parker.

Nate did, shoes and all.

"Now git on up with me."

Parker went up quickly. Nate took longer, because

he stopped to stare at J.E.B. Stuart, who'd waited obe-
diently and now came forward to inspect the newcomer.

"Can you use a Winchester?" asked Parker. "I got
two .44s. One of 'em's for you."

Nate seemed to fidget some before he replied, "No.
The Widow Bybee didn't hold with guns. My father
didn't either."

"I'll teach ya then. Funny kinda pa you had." Parker
urged the team out from the shadows, and as he did
Nate, who was fumbling for his shoes, saw the coffin
for the first time by moonlight.

"What's that back there?" he cried out.

"What's it look like? It's a buryin' box I got this
mornin' at the undertaker's. Git back there with it,
and lay down so's nobody'll see ya leavin' town."

"No!" cried Nate Graber. "Are you going to kill
somebody? Is that why you've got Winchesters? That's
a coffin!"

Parker laughed, then explained his errand to Nate,
who sat petrified beside him. "All right, if you're scared,
don' git back there, Graber. Naw, I don' have it in
mind to shoot nobody I don' have to shoot."

Finally he saw Nate relax and nod. "So you're going
up to this Whiskey Creek after your brother?"

"Yep."

"That's what my father would have done, Parker. It's
the right thing to do."

"Nate, you sure talk queer," said Parker Quiney, as

31

they passed through Cottonwood without one challenge from the saloon-bound men on the street. "Where do ya hail from?"

"East Texas."

"I never been there—not even to Fort Worth," said Parker. It eased him to know Graber was a Texan, too. Making talk, he asked, "Ya been to school, Nate?"

"Oh, yes," said the other boy. "I'm in the ninth grade. I was put ahead a year." He looked at Parker. "You must have gone to some other school, maybe at Tucker Springs. I never saw you once in Cottonwood."

Parker chuckled. "I ain't never been to school a'tall. None a us Quineys got no use for wisdom bringers."

"Can't you read or write, Parker?"

"Not one word, 'cept for my name. Nerissa, she's my sister-in-law, showed me how to do that. I say there ain't no point in book learnin'."

Nate was silent for a time, then suddenly he changed the subject. "I've got a five-dollar gold piece my father gave me and six bits, Parker."

"That's more'n I've got. You can buy yerself a hat with the six bits. I throwed yer old one away. I got two dollars and two bits." Suddenly Parker spied the black-and-white flash of J.E.B. Stuart as he darted off the dirt road after a jackrabbit. "You fool animal. Come on back here," he called out. Then he whistled and yelled, "Git back here, J.E.B. Stuart."

Nate Graber said very quickly, "That's a strange name for a dog. Why's he called that?"

Parker's reply was proud. "Before he got kicked by a horse and died a lockjaw, my pa was in the Confed'rate Army. He admired old Gen'ral Stuart so much us Quineys always had us a dog named after him."

"Oh."

Parker thought Nate's "oh" was a pretty cold sort of thing to say about his dog. "You don' take kindly to dogs, Nate?"

"The Widow Bybee wouldn't have any cats or dogs in her house." Nate's voice was hard.

"You mad at me because a what I did to yer purty hat, Nate?" asked Parker, mystified at this sudden change.

"No." The one word sounded all wrong, like somebody'd yelled it down a deep well, thought Parker Quiney.

"You think the widow'll send somebody after ya, Nate?" he asked.

"Maybe." The answer was gloomy. "The court pays her three dollars a month to keep me. I never told her about my gold piece, or she would have taken it away from me."

"Well, if somebody she sends catches up with ya, it'll be all yer fault," warned Parker Quiney. "Ya wouldn' do what I told ya'—git in back with the box and lay down. Somebody who knows ya coulda seen ya headin' north and go tell her."

"I know that very well." Again the words came from the bottom of a well.

2
The
Gospel
Shark

There was no sound but the chink of the harness as Pilgrim and Hooraw followed the wagon ruts northward. Parker glanced once or twice at Nate Graber as they went along, wondering if he'd made a mistake. Maybe he should a picked somebody else to keep him company. Take that bus'ness of not hiding in back with the coffin. Nate should a done that for his own good. It was beginnin' to look like this Graber kid didn't know a heifer from a horned frog—even if he did come from Texas.

34

Before long they came to the Colorado River, flowing eastward. Parker turned off the road, jolting the wagon to a spot under some trees. Here he stopped the team. "We'll cross over in the mornin'," he said.

Nate nodded his head, his pale ringlets fluttering in the chilly night wind. "You think nobody will be coming after me until then?" he asked.

Parker only grunted. Just as soon as he could get his hands on some shears he was going to do something about Graber's hair. "Did the widow make you have them curls? You hanker after keepin' 'em?"

"I hate them!"

Parker laughed as he started to unhitch the horses. He'd tie them to the wagon wheel, not hobble them tonight. There wasn' any point in chasin' after 'em at daybreak, not if they wanted a real head start on somebody the widow might be sendin'. Maybe she'd never find out which way Nate'd lit out or who he'd gone with. Parker was almost willing to bet his precious Lone Star boots that few men who might have seen them leaving Cottonwood would tell on Nate.

"There's some cornbread and some slab bacon in one a them sacks, kid," he told Nate. "We ain't makin' no fire tonight. We'll be sleepin' under the wagon."

"All right, Parker." Nate Graber threw his blankets and Parker's bedroll onto the grass, and asked, "How far is the next town?"

"That'd be Lockville. Thirty miles north, I reckon.

I ain't never been there. I ain't never been outa this county or north a this river. I don' even know where this here river goes."

"Oh, it flows to the Gulf of Mexico. It rises in West Texas," Nate said precisely. Then he added, "How long will we be gone?"

"I dunno. Six weeks—two months. That oughta give ya time to have a rest from the widow, huh?"

Nate spoke eagerly. "That would give me time to teach you to read and write, Parker. I helped teach the smaller children at school, so I know how."

From the wagon wheel where he was tying the team, Parker said, "I can't see a man needs it to be a rough-string rider."

"Everybody ought to be able to do those things!" protested Nate Graber.

"I told you I can't see no need for it to herd cow brutes or bust broncs. Don't keep at me about it unless you want your wishbone scratched up plenty." Before Nate could say anything else, Parker started whistling for J.E.B. Stuart. He'd tie him up, too. There wasn' any call for the dog to be out chasin' jacks two nights in a row.

They forded the Colorado at daybreak at what Parker judged was the most shallow place, one where he could see some rocks sticking out of the yellow-brown water. As it was, the water came high enough

36

on the wheels for Nate to reach down nervously and touch it.

"Is it warmer'n it was when we got baptized in it?" asked Parker.

"A little bit." Nate sighed with relief as the team plodded onto the opposite bank. "I thought for a while there the water would flood the wagon and maybe your team would have to swim."

Parker shook his head. "Nope. I reckoned right about this ford and didn' git us into no boghole. But there'll be a couple more rivers to cross before we git where I'm goin'." He eyed the other boy's yellow curls without much enthusiasm. He certainly hadn't liked Nate's nervousness at this first fording. "You know what it means in Texas when somebody says 'He's a good man to ride a river with'?"

"No."

Parker Quiney sighed. "I didn't reckon ya would. It means you got pure grit in ya. There ain't nothin more dangerous than ridin' rivers with a trail herd." He clucked to Hooraw and Pilgrim as they reached high ground. Wet from his swim, J.E.B. Stuart went dashing past the team in pursuit of a road runner. Parker asked casually, his eyes on the dog, "Nate, what'd your pa do anyhow?"

"Oh, he was a schoolteacher before he went to Mexico mining."

Parker groaned aloud. "A wisdom bringer. I mighta

knowed it by how you talk." He added thoughtfully, "I never heard tell a one a 'em having a lotta grit."

"My pa had plenty of it!" flared Nate. Then, in a sadder tone, he said, "Everybody in Cottonwood thinks he's dead down there in Durango. I haven't heard from him for so long I think he must be, too. My mother died a long time ago in Mexico."

This information surprised Parker. "You savvy Spanish, Nate?"

"Yes, I do."

"Well, I don' think that'll do you much good where we're goin'. It'd be better if you savvied some Indian talk mebbe."

"Parker, how did your mother die?" asked Nate.

"Folks said she was plumb tuckered out and jest laid down and died after Pa did. There was twelve a us alive then. Now Jesse's gone, so there's only eleven."

"That's certainly a lot of you Quineys."

"And only one a you, huh? Well, it don' matter. We're both leppies all the same. Know what they are?"

"Orphans, I imagine." For a moment Nate was silent, then he said, "Thank you for taking me along with you, Parker. I couldn't have stood it much longer with the widow. I want you to know how much I appreciate it. I hope you'll find me good enough to ride a river with."

"I hope so, too, Nate. I'll be watchin' ya. Jest remember, I'm pretty positive about everybody I meet. Come on, let's stop a spell an' eat the rest of old Nerissa's cornbread. It'll be beans and skillet corn dodgers after that's gone. Can you cook?" Parker swung the chestnut and the white horse out of the deep wheel ruts to the left.

Even though Nate was clinging to the seat with both hands to keep from being pitched out, he answered, "Some. I learned a little from my father and more from the widow. She said she thought men ought to have accomplishments, too."

"Hum," said Parker. "That's good. I don' cook myself."

Once they had cornbread in hand, there was quiet again. Parker noticed, though, how often Nate glanced uneasily behind him at the coffin. Guessing the other boy's thoughts, he said warningly, "I'm gonna fetch that box up to Whiskey Creek or bust a hamstring. Earl's sendin' me to do it. Us Quineys are hogs for duty!"

Privately Parker Quiney was sure of several things as they came into Lockville at noon of the next day. Graber didn't know much about horses even if he was a passable fryer and corn dodger maker. Another thing was that nobody seemed to be followin' him, and the third thing was that Nate was too quiet to be much company. The immediate problem, however, was that Hooraw had thrown a shoe.

"We're gonna have to hunt up a blacksmith in Lockville," Parker told Nate when he noticed the big chestnut going sore-footed and got down to lift up his front hoof. "This'll cost us a half dollar, for sure, but a smart man looks after his horses first." Parker intended to start educating Graber in the important things he ought to know.

Lockville was a lot like Cottonwood except it didn't have so many trees around, and it was dustier. Parker spied a courthouse and jail in the main square and passed them by. Blacksmiths favored one end of a town or the other. He stopped the team, listened for the sound of a hammer, and headed toward it with Hooraw limping.

"There's a blacksmith ahead." Nate pointed to a sign.

"Yep, sure is," agreed Parker, who drove up to the shop, leaped down, and went inside, where the smith's fire burned red in the blackness. He tried to peer through the rising steam the smith made as he dipped a piece of glowing iron into a tub of water beside his forge, but he couldn't see a thing.

"I got a horse outside that's throwed a shoe," he said to the steam.

"Fetch the critter in," came a husky voice.

Parker gaped as the steam cleared. The blacksmith wasn' no man at all. He was a *her*—the biggest, widest woman Parker allowed he'd ever seen. She wore a leather apron, a man's striped shirt, and cowboy hat. "Ma'am?" his voice quavered.

The lady smith chuckled. "That's me, Adelina Symonds. Fetch in that hoss a yers."

40

Shaking his head, Parker went out. "Come on down from there," he told Nate, as he unhitched Hooraw. "You gotta see what I just seen."

Leading the chestnut and followed by J.E.B. Stuart, the two boys went into the shop. Now it was Nate's turn to gawk at the strange sight.

"Light somewheres, you longhaired yellow-head," said the woman after she'd lifted up Hooraw's hoof to check it for size. "You"—she singled out Parker— "work them bellows fer me while I heat up a shoe for yer critter." She grinned at the boys. "Where you hail from?"

"Fort Worth," Parker lied, to cover Nate's trail.

"Travelin' alone?" she asked.

"Yes," said Nate from where he sat on a barrel.

She gave him a tight smile. "Run away from home, I betcha?"

Parker said, "No, ma'am, we're bound on a errand."

"How far ya goin'?"

"Up to Ruination."

She shot them both a sharp glance. "On the road to Ruination, huh?"

"Yes'm."

"I bet if you ain't runnin' away you'd be orphans."

"Yes, we're leppies, Miss Symonds," said Nate.

"*Mrs.* Symonds," she corrected him. "My husband's a preacher hereabouts." Then she asked, "What kinda errand you on, kids?"

Parker thought the lady blacksmith was friendly,

and she liked to talk, which was more'n he could say for Nate Graber. "To bring back my brother Jesse. He's gone and got hisself killed."

"Land a mercy!" she dropped her hammer onto the floor, then bent puffing to pick it up. "Who'd send colts like you on a errand like that?"

"My brother Earl."

"He oughta be horsewhipped." Then she said, grabbing the bellows' handle from Parker and pumping it furiously, "I don' believe a word of it."

"It's true," volunteered Nate. "We've got a coffin in the wagon outside."

Mrs. Symonds left the bellows' handle to Parker, strode outside, and looked in the wagon back. "By the word of all that's holy, there it is!" Parker heard her exclaim in wonder.

When she came back in a rustle of leather skirts, she said nothing for a time while Hooraw's shoe heated in the coals. Finally she came out with, "You musta been travelin' for a long time if you come all the way here from Fort Worth. How'd you like to stay the night at my house and have a fried-chicken supper?"

"I'd like that," said Nate, who looked appealingly at Parker.

"Sure, ma'am." Then Parker asked, "What'll it cost fer the shoe? We ain't got much cash money."

"Not a cent—not fer fryin'-size kids like you who got a errand like that one to do. How about doin' a little favor for me, though?"

"Glad to, ma'am," answered Parker.

"Go git my husband outa the Union House and bring him here."

"What's that?" asked Nate.

"A drinkin' saloon!"

"What's a minister doing in there?" exclaimed Graber.

She laughed at the question. "Preachin'—not drinkin'."

J.E.B. Stuart nosing ahead of them, the boys left the blacksmith's shop. "You sure jawed a lot back there, Nate," accused Parker. "If I hadn't thought quick, ya'd told her ya was from Cottonwood sure. First, ya don't talk at all to me, and then ya talk too much to her."

"She was friendly to me," said Nate, not looking at Parker.

Parker let this remark pass. He asked, "Nate, I bet ya ain't never been in a saloon before."

"I haven't. Have you?"

"A couple a times with Earl before Nerissa put a stop to it. Saloons ain't like church. A man keeps his hat on in there. I sure wish you had yerself one to hide under."

Together they mounted the steps of the Union House and went through the swinging doors. Nobody, and there must have been two dozen men in there, paid them or the dog a bit of heed. They all sat glumly at tables or stood gloomily at the bar, listening to the man who was shouting at them. "Vipers! Down to the depths of perdition you shall go! You're rattling your way past the Pearly Gates to Hell. Ruination. Ruination!"

Parker stared hard at the orator, aware of Nate's gasp. The man was good-size, his face was scarlet from bellowing, and his eyes were a piercing frost-blue. He wore a black frock coat, but no hat. On the table before him lay a Bible and a gun. Now he reached for his hogleg and banged on the wood with its barrel for attention. "You quit that shiftin' around, you varmints. Harken to my words, you black-souled sinners." And he was off again in a stampede of words.

"He's a for sure gospel shark," whispered Parker to Nate. "I reckon that'd be Preacher Symonds who's headin' down the glory trail."

"I wonder what kind of church he has?" said Nate uneasily.

"Gospel sharks don't gen'rally have churches, Earl says. They take up preachin' on their own."

"How will we get him to notice us, Parker?"

"We fire off a six-shooter like his—if we got one—or we yell louder'n he does. Like this." Parker's higher voice rose to its fullest. "Hey, Preacher. Yer wife wants ya!"

The big man stopped in the middle of a flowing sentence, picked up his gun, and put it into his holster. "Who'd you buttons be?" he asked, sounding mighty annoyed.

Parker dodged the question. "Yer wife's shoein' my horse. She sent us to git ya."

"I'm a comin'." Preacher Symonds got his Bible and followed the boys outside while the men in the Union House laughed. One called after him, "Git on home, or your missus'll dust yer britches for ya."

The gospel shark turned around to shake his fist and shout in return. "The devil'll come take you away, sinner!" At a slow pace the preacher led the way. "What does Adelina want?"

"I dunno," said Parker. Then before the preacher could ask them their names again, he told of his errand and that they were orphans from Fort Worth. "Yer wife asked us to supper."

"Commendable of her, very commendable," said the man.

Dropping behind his bulk, Parker whispered to Nate, "They're gonna be after knowin' our names next. Who you wanta be? I reckon I'll be Sam Houston Smith."

Nate thought for a moment. "I'll be Ulysses S. Johnson."

Parker gave him a disgusted look. "That ain't no Texas name."

"All the same, that's who I'm going to be."

At the shop Mrs. Symonds had Hooraw's shoe ready to be nailed on. As she passed Parker with the rasp to file down the chestnut's hoof to fit the shoe, the boy asked her, "Ma'am, have you got any shears?"

"Uh-huh, I cut up some tin sometimes or trim a

critter's tail if it gits in my way. They're hangin' on the wall." She jerked her head to the right.

"Light on that there barrel agin," ordered Parker. The preacher nodded as Parker went toward Nate with the heavy shears. "Vanity is sin," he droned. "Shear the lamb of his vanity, boy."

Nate eyed Parker doubtfully and seemed to shrink a little.

"I ain't gonna scalp ya or roach yer mane. Quit hunkerin' down so much," said Parker Quiney. "Anyhow if ya don' like the job I do, ya can git a hat here in Lockville."

As Preacher Symonds held Hooraw's bridle and spoke very softly to his wife between blows of her hammer, Parker went to work on Nate's golden curls.

For a blacksmith, Parker had to admit Mrs. Preacher Symonds was sure some cook. That'd been the best fried chicken and gravy and grits he'd ever had. "Thank ya, ma'am, for the feed and shoein' my horse," he told her, remembering his manners, though he was thinking all the time she had a face built for a hackamore if he'd ever seen one. Her gray hair was short as a man's—shorter even than Nate's now and it didn' look much better neither.

"You was sayin' there's eleven of you Smiths?" she asked Parker.

"Yep, there was so many when my biggest brother

46

took us anywheres outside town and stopped so he could git some peace and quiet, he used to picket us each on a rope to stakes a good ways apart. That stopped us from killin' each other."

The woman laughed. "All redheaded, I bet."

"Ever' one a us, ma'am."

All at once the preacher asked from the top of the table, "Was your pa in the war?"

"He sure was," said Parker. "He was in the Confed'rate Army."

"Do tell," commented Mrs. Symonds, who'd turned to Nate. "What about your pa, Ulysses?"

Parker saw Nate across from him draw a deep breath. "My father wasn't in either army. He went to Mexico in 1861."

"How come? Was he scared for his hide?" demanded Parker Quiney.

Nate scowled at Parker. "No, he wasn't! He wasn't afraid of anything, I told you. He didn't like slavery, and he didn't want Texas to secede from the Union, and he didn't like war." The words tumbled out of Nate. "He and Mama went to Mexico from East Texas so their vigilante neighbors wouldn't come at night and hang them like they did some of our friends. Lots of people from our part of the state went away then and only came back home when the war was over."

Shocked, Parker gawked at Nate. "Then you're a *Yankee!*" Parker felt his face growing hot as his anger

47

grew. "And I was fool enough to take to ya and fetch ya with me." He snorted loudly. "You're a damyankee!"

Preacher Symonds said calmly, "Hold on, boy. Me and my wife wasn't in Texas neither. We went to California in '61."

"You're Yankees, too?" accused Parker Quiney.

"I would have chosen the Union side if I had not been what I am, a man of God. Preachers don't take sides and fight in wars. I have a gun solely to intimidate varmints." He pushed back his chair. "You colts git on up to bed now. You might as well spend the night here. We got the room."

Still glaring at Nate, Parker didn't see the man wink at his wife. Parker arose and pointed to Nate. "I'm gettin' rid a you tomorrer mornin'. I'm sleepin' in the barn tonight—not anyplace with you, scrub!"

Nate, his face gone pale, sat silent while Parker made for the kitchen door. The preacher blocked his way, spreading out his long arms. "Peace be unto you, lads. The war's a long time over. There's a feather bed upstairs. Tonight you'll share it like brothers. I'll have no fightin' in my house."

Parker eyed the man. He was as big as Earl and looked as strong so he turned about, frowning, and made for the hallway stairs. Nate met him at the bottom and clumped up beside him.

"Second door at the top of the steps," sang out Mrs. Symonds, cheery as a meadowlark.

The preacher saw them all the way up, opened the door for them, and showed them inside. "Good night," he told them, as they turned to face him.

An instant later they heard him turn the key in the lock.

Nate was nearest and so first to grab the doorknob and rattle it. "We're locked in! Hey, let us out!" he shouted.

"Glory Hallelujah, I've got you scalawags safe and sound now!" came the man's voice outside. "Safe and sound from peril and sin here in my house. You'll stay in there 'til the folks come from the orphans' home in Polkstown for you."

"But I got to git to Whiskey Creek!" Parker came rushing to the door to kick it open. "I don't want to go to no leppies' home, you old sin buster!"

"There never was a Texas-bred boy yet who couldn't benefit from a good Christian home. I'm takin' your team and wagon and pot-hound dog to the sheriff," rumbled the preacher. "Sleep tight, boys. You can't break that door down. It's solid oak, and Adelina made the hinges herself. It'll bust off yer toes. You're all done with traipsin' across Texas, runnin' away."

This speech made Parker wisely draw back his foot. He glanced over his shoulder at Nate, who'd gone to sit on the big four-poster bed and said, "That's right, jest sit there like a wart on a pickle, you scrub." Parker went to look hopefully over the kerosene lamp out the window. No, there wasn' any tree handy, and it was a long leg-bustin' way to the ground. Pondering, he started to sing through his teeth, "My parson's a wolf on his pulpit of bones. . . ."

"We have to get out of here," Nate interrupted him.

Parker Quiney whirled on him angrily. "You got that much sense, huh?"

"If I can think of a way out of here, Parker, will you still take me with you even if I am a Yankee?"

Parker snorted. "Sure. All you got to do is figger out a way fer me to git to the sheriff."

Nate looked startled. "Sheriff? He'll hold us for the orphans' home, too, or give us back to the Symondses, won't he?"

"Mebbe not. The way I reckon, the sheriff here'll prob'ly be somebody outa the Texas Rangers, like Earl was. Mebbe he fought Comanches alongside my brother. Lotsa sheriffs done that."

"All right, Parker." Nate rolled over on the bed, deliberately putting his shoes on the quilt. He rested his head on his cupped hands, looking at the ceiling. "I'm starting to think."

All that night and the next day it seemed to Parker Quiney that Nate thought, now and then muttering to himself. But for all of his thinking, Nate pitched right good into the victuals Mrs. Preacher Symonds brought up to them. Parker didn't have any stomach for her grub anymore.

In his stocking feet he paced, stopping often to peer

out the small window at the street below. He'd decided it wouldn't do any good to bust the glass with a chair and yell for help. Preacher Symonds and his blacksmith wife were known in Lockville, while he and Nate hadn't even used their real names. There wasn' no use in rushin' the door when Mrs. Symonds came up with the chuck neither. Two fryin'-size boys couldn' stand up to her or her husband. Each of 'em plumb filled up the whole doorway.

After supper of the second day Nate sat up suddenly and announced, "I think I know what we ought to do, Parker."

"What's that?" Parker stopped in midprowl.

"Mrs. Symonds is downstairs now, isn't she?"

"I reckon so—doin' dishes if she don' leave 'em for that gospel shark to do. What you got in mind?"

"Settin' a fire in here." Nate pointed to the kerosene lamp.

"Holy Gatlins!" exploded Parker. "You'll burn us up! What good'll that do?"

"Well," reflected Nate, "it can do a lot of good— if we do it just right."

"How'll we do that?"

"Take down the curtains here, pile them on the bare floor in a corner away from the door and bed, pour some kerosene on them out of the lamp, and set fire to them."

Parker took off his hat and tousled his hair. "We're locked in, remember?"

"Oh, I know that. All we have to do is yell 'Fire' at the door and out the window. If somebody hears us outside first, they'll make Mrs. Symonds or the preacher let us out. If they hear us, they'll come up to see about the furniture. Then we skin out past them while they're thinking about the fire—not us."

"But what if nobody hears, and we ain't able to put out the fire ourselves, Nate?"

"We jump out the window."

"We'll prob'ly have to go to that there orphans' home then with busted legs!"

"It's better than burning up in here." Nate fell back onto the bed. "Think it over, Parker."

Parker thought, hauled on his boots, and then went to the window to reach for the curtains. "I'll do this here work. I'm taller'n ya are. You take care a the kerosene." As Nate went across to the lamp, Parker Quiney muttered, "Holy Gatlins, settin' fires! Now I see how the damyankees won the war."

Firing the curtains took only a moment or so. When they started blazing and Nate had thrown on a feather pillow, Parker went to the door and hollered and pounded with his fists and boots. Nate broke the window with a chair and howled out it, "Help!" For half a minute the boys bellowed, then stopped for breath, coughing in the smoke.

"Anybody listenin' to us below?" asked Parker.

"I didn't see anybody down there," replied Nate. "Can you hear anybody coming up the steps?"

Parker put his ear to the door, the smoke billowing about him. "Somebody sure is. Get ready!"

Soon they heard the click of the key, then the door was flung open. The blacksmith stood there, looking worried. When she saw the flames and smoke, her eyes widened with horror. Ignoring the boys, she dashed into the room and jerked her fancy hand-sewed quilt off the bed.

Parker didn't wait to see what valuable thing she'd save next. He ran past her, out onto the landing with Nate behind him. Together they clattered down the stairs and to the front door. As Nate ran on ahead, Parker stopped in the parlor for an instant, then joined him out on the porch. There they halted. Men, carrying buckets, were coming at them from all directions. One called out, "Where's the fire?"

"Upstairs!" shouted Parker, leaping off the porch, heading toward the town square. Then all at once he saw the preacher looming up out of the twilight. Parker grabbed Nate by the jacket and pulled him behind somebody's buckboard. When the big man had passed, the boys started running again.

Parker and Nate burst open the front door of the jailhouse and stood panting until the dark-browed, lean sheriff looked up from his chair. "What d'ya kids want?" he demanded.

"My team and wagon and Winchesters and supplies," came from Parker.

"And his dog," added Nate.

The sheriff nodded. "You'd be that Smith boy then, from Fort Worth, the one hell-roarer Symonds is keepin' for the man from the orphans' home?"

"No, I *ain't* no Smith!" Parker shouted, pulling off his hat. "I'm from near Cottonwood. I'm Parker Quiney."

The sheriff smiled. "Yeah, you're a Quiney brass monkey, all right. It's writ all over you, redhead."

"I sure am. You know my brother Earl? You know Jesse?" Parker rattled off the names of all of the older Quineys.

"I courted one a your sisters a couple years back until she slipped me the mitten. What're you doin' here in Lockville? Who's this here with you?"

"Ulysses S. Johnson. He's from Cottonwood, too." Then Parker told the sheriff of his business and of the preacher's treachery. "So I ain't, truthful speakin', got *no* family," he finished with a gesture toward Nate. "He's got family, too. His pa's in Mexico minin'. You give us back my team and all, huh?"

The sheriff's face was somber. "I'm sorry to hear about your brother. I don't see no reason not to let you have the team. I never heard tell of a Santa Rosa County Quiney to be a flannelmouth yet. And I've knowed the preacher to be a liar now and then." The man got up and took a ring of keys down from some deer antlers. "I'll get your dog out first."

"He's in jail?" asked Nate, shocked.

"Can't you hear him barking in there? How else'd

54

anybody keep that animal less'n he was along with me?" said Parker scornfully. He handed Nate the thing he'd paused for in the Symondses parlor, the black-smith's big brown hat. "Here, didn't I say I'd git ya a hat, Graber?"

"But it's a lady's!" Nate protested.

"It ain't neither. It's a man's. Besides, she wasn' no lady far as I can see."

Doubtfully Nate stuck the hat on his shorn head. "It's too big, Parker."

"Yep, it is. But yer ears'll hold it up jest fine."

Nate looked at Parker as J.E.B. Stuart came happily from the cells in the next room and jumped up on his master. "I guess this hat means you'll keep your promise to take me with you then?"

"Quineys don't go back on their word," Parker told him as the sheriff returned, "but, Graber, let me tell you one thing. I figger you and me are prob'ly gonna git along like two bobcats in a gunnysack." The boy turned to the sheriff. "Can we git on our way right now? We got some time to make up."

"Don't see no reason to keep you," said the man. He scribbled on some paper and gave it to Parker. "Your team's at the livery stable. This is a note to them." He unlocked a cupboard while Parker handed the paper to Nate and said, gesturing toward the cupboard, "Take what's yours in here, boys."

They divided the sacks of food and each took a Quiney Winchester. Then, stuffing the box of ammunition into his jacket pocket, Parker asked, "Where's my coffin?"

"In the wagon—far as I know."

"Much obliged to ya, sheriff," said Parker Quiney, ready to go.

"Thank you very much, too," echoed Nate Graber.

As Nate went out at Parker's heels, he bumped into a newly arrived deputy, who called out from the doorway, "There was a fire over at the sin buster's—not much a one, though. Folks got it put out fast."

"Come on, Nate!" Parker hissed to him outside. "We got to git away while we can. If old hell-roarer Symonds or his missus gits their hands on us now they won' give us no more chance of gittin away from 'em next time than a white hen at a prayer meetin' a coyotes!"

3

The Seminole Elixir

With J.E.B. Stuart running ahead of the wagon, Parker and Nate left Lockville as fast as they could. For several moonlit miles Parker forced the team to run, then pulled the horses to a steady strong trot.

They hadn't had any trouble getting Hooraw and Pilgrim and the wagon returned to them, and they'd found the coffin just as they'd left it. The nighthawk livery-stable man hadn't turned a hair when he'd read the sheriff's note. He had helped Parker hitch up the horses and fill their water buckets while Nate had stowed away their supplies.

Over the steady clanking sound of their horses' harness, Parker told Nate, "We're gonna travel all night. We'll hole up somewheres off the road tomorrer." He looked at Nate's big-hat silhouette. "I reckon you had enough of layin' aroun' on top of a feather bed, huh?"

Nate said, "Yes. I guess you've had plenty of walking around back and forth in your stocking feet, too?"

Parker grunted his reply. "It feels good to settle my backside on a wagon seat agin. You didn' expect me to walk aroun' in my boots while I was thinkin', did ya? Cowboys don' walk nowheres they don' have to. That's what horses is for."

"Why don't they walk?" Nate sounded annoyed.

"They jes' don'. Besides it ain't so easy walkin' in high heels."

"If that's so," Nate asked, "why don't you get some sensible shoes, Parker?"

"Sensible shoes!" mocked the redheaded boy loudly, making Pilgrim prick up his ears and leap forward nervously. "Like them sodbuster things a yers?"

"Yes."

Parker spoke softly so he wouldn't make Pilgrim more skittish. "I'll git ya some real boots later on."

"No!"

"Holy Snakes, why not? Mine's got Lone Stars on 'em. It's the kind bronc snappers wear."

"I've seen them." Nate's voice was cold. "I don't want boots like yours. You cut my hair and got me a new hat. Haven't you done enough?"

"I was only doin' ya favors. Don' tell me you liked that there bonnet with the ribbons on it and them curls?"

"No, I didn't, but I'd have got rid of that hat the widow made me wear myself. And I'd have gone to a barber. Don't do me any more good turns, Parker Quiney, without my asking you!"

Wounded, Parker muttered, "You bet I won't. I musta been loco to promise to take you to Whiskey Creek with me. I dunno why I oughta keep a promise to a Yankee."

"Well, don't you think for one minute I'd have wasted any deep thinking on how to get a Rebel out of a locked room if I wasn't locked in with him!"

There was an angry silence between the two boys for a mile. Then Nate broke it as they passed a lone mesquite, a black shadow beside the trail. "The Widow Bybee's maybe sent somebody after me already. Maybe the minister'll send riders, too. He doesn't have to let the sheriff in Lockville know he's doing it. That orphans' home is in Polkstown. I don't know anybody in Polkstown who could help us, do you?"

"Nope, I don' reckon I do. It's in a county where no Quiney I know about ever's gone to. We're gettin' outa Quiney hill country fast now."

Nate muttered, "I suppose we ought to stick together for a while then?"

Parker agreed grudgingly, "If I can put up with a scrub like you."

Nate was so annoyed he burst out, "Maybe I'll find a place I like along the way and leave before we get to Ruination and Whiskey Creek, Parker Quiney."

"Mebbe, scrub, you'll leave a long time afore that!"

At dawn, without having seen another wagon or a rider, Parker turned the team off across flat ground. He headed the horses for a thicket and entered through an opening, stopping in a place where there was a little brush. "This here cedar brake'll do to hide us," he told Nate. "We'll git us some chuck and then some shut-eye. We won' make no fire. We'll start out agin later on near to sunset."

"It'll have to be hardtack and water from the bucket like prisoners have," said Nate, staring mournfully into the sky, as a raven flapped his way out of the brake.

"You lined yer flue plenty with Symonds chuck. Goin' hungry now won' hurt ya," accused Parker. "Tomorrer ya can cook beans and corn dodgers."

Nate sighed and crawled into the back of the wagon to rummage in the supplies. Unhitching Pilgrim, Parker watched the fat boy in the too-large hat, noticing how carefully he moved about so as not to touch the coffin. Parker Quiney sighed in exasperation.

In spite of the noise of the thicket birds and the whirring insects the boys slept under the wagon until late in the afternoon. Then they crawled out, ate again, and headed toward the trail. J.E.B. Stuart bounded ahead, happy to be away from the brake, where Parker had kept him tied, whining, to a wagon wheel.

"Look at that dog go!" Parker told Nate. "He sure didn't cotton to bein' kept in no jailhouse."

"I don't see why the sheriff put him in a cell at all, Parker," said the other boy.

Parker scoffed. "J.E.B.'s a fancy kinda dog and worth cash money. Other folks like him. You don' take to him 'cause he's named after a Confed'rate general."

"I like the dog even if I don't like his name, although I wouldn't say he's very obedient."

Parker ignored Nate. J.E.B. Stuart had flushed a jack from under a large cactus. With a yelp of pure joy he was off and away in pounding pursuit of the leaping rabbit. In a twinkling the black-and-white flash had disappeared from sight into another brake.

"Someday you're going to lose him rabbit chasing," predicted Nate gloomily.

"Nope, I can always tell by his yapping where he is!"

A moment later the dog's happy barking changed to an ear-splitting yelp. Parker didn't hesitate. He pulled the team to a halt, handed the reins to Nate, grabbed his Winchester, and leaped down. "You stay here, Graber. My dog's in trouble!" Running, the boy bored through the brush to the source of the shrill cries, paused only an instant, raised the rifle, and pulled the trigger.

The thick-bodied brown snake, coiled to strike a second time, jerked up into the air when the Winchester's heavy bullet smashed into it, then lay twitching as Parker hurried to the dog.

61

He kneeled beside him. "You got bit, J.E.B.?" asked the boy tenderly. Then he saw the blood on the white fur of the dog's upper leg. "Oh, Lord!" he added softly. He shifted his rifle to under his left arm and scooped up J.E.B. Stuart with his right. Staggering under the animal's weight, Parker Quiney made his way back to the waiting wagon two hundred yards distant.

"He's been snakebit, Nate. Let the team graze. They won' go far. We got to help old J.E.B.!"

Nate's face blanched, but he jumped down from the seat and kneeled beside Parker, who laid the dog gently on the grass. "I'm sure sorry, Parker."

Parker nodded, taking out his knife. "Nate, you hold him down while I work on him. Don' let him jerk around too much."

Nate held the whimpering, struggling dog while Parker swiftly cut deep into J.E.B.'s shoulder. Next he put his mouth to the wound sucking out the poison, spitting the venom and blood onto the grass.

Suddenly Nate said, "I'll suck some, too, if you want."

Parker wiped his bloody mouth with his sleeve. "It might make ya throw up. Besides I'm near done." And he spat again.

"But I'm willing to anyway, Parker."

"There ain't no cause to. This here's a Quiney dog. I'll look after him. You go fetch the horses." Parker put the dog into the back of the wagon next to the coffin.

When they were back up on the seat, Nate asked, "Parker, do you think he'll live?"

Parker shook his head. "I don' know. A rattler that big can kill a full-growed steer if he fangs him in the wrong place. We could use a chicken to draw the pizen out. Earl says a split-up chicken does the job jes fine fer water-moccasin bites. But there ain't no hens around here on the prairie."

"What are we going to do, Parker?"

"Keep goin'. I done all I could for J.E.B. For sure, we can't go back."

The dog lay motionless as they traveled the next half mile in spite of Nate's whistling attempts to get him to prick up his ears and show some signs of life. Just before sunset Parker came to a halt. The road forked. One fork led northeast, the other northwest along a line of mesquite trees. "Which one'll I take?" he asked himself.

Then Nate shouted, "There's a chicken over there!"

Parker looked to where Nate pointed. There was something white walking along the northwest road. "Holy Gatlins, it *is* a chicken!" Parker brought the reins down on Hooraw's and Pilgrim's backs with a sharp slap, plunging them into a quick trot. Then he gave the reins to Nate again and jumped down out of the rolling wagon. "I'm gonna git that hen. You musta been prayin' for one to come along!" he yelled to Nate and stumbled ahead.

The "hen" wasn't a hen, but a rooster. As Parker

soon found, it was a fast, wary bird. It fled before him, flapping and squawking, zigzagging across the road. At last, just as the team came abreast of him, he caught it, flinging himself down on top of the rooster at the side of the road. Holding it by the legs with its head down, he got up and shouted triumphantly over its cries, "I got the—"

"No, *chico,* you did not. It is mine!" A cold hiss of a voice interrupted him. As he gaped, the rooster dangling, a woman came out of the bright-green mesquite across from him. She leveled a double-barrelled shotgun at his chest. She was beautiful, tall and thin with golden skin and long golden earrings. Parker stared open-mouthed at her glittering black eyes and long black hair, purple shawl, and scarlet skirt. A Mexican gal if he'd ever seen one!

He let the rooster drop and put up both hands. Then he heard Nate's quick Spanish from the wagon and saw the woman lower the gun. He watched her turn toward Nate, walking slowly, and climb gracefully on the wheel to peer inside.

"Madre de Dios, es verdad!" Parker heard her exclaim. Then she spoke to Nate again and he to her. Shaking her sleek head, she got down, pointed to the brake ahead of them, and let out another flood of Spanish.

"What's she sayin'?" demanded Parker.

"The coffin surprised her and so did your dog. She says to follow her. She says chickens don't help one bit with rattlesnake bites like they do with moccasin bites, but she knows something that will." Nate was smiling. "Mexicans know how to cure snakebites with milkweed. She says there's some around here. She says for you not to worry about your dog, because she's a witch from Chihuahua."

"Glory Hallelujah!" Parker murmured twice as he lurched along in the ruts beside Hooraw. A witch? He'd never run across a witch before.

The woman led them into the brush for a distance, then stopped, pointing. Parker saw a tall, narrow wagon in front of him. It was covered over, like a house on wheels, and painted red with gilt decorations. He knew it right off for a medicine show wagon, like one he'd seen before in Tucker Springs.

As they came up to the wagon Nate halted the team after much wheezing effort and shouting "Whoa."

Parker hissed to him, "What do the signs on the wagon say?"

Nate read the shiny curling letters out loud, " 'Dr. Augustus Romulus Tyree, Professor of the Occult Sciences.' Below his name it says 'Madame Maria, World Famous Occultiste' and under her name 'Sole Proprietors in the Western Hemisphere of the Wonderful Seminole Elixir'."

Parker would have asked what that all meant except that the Mexican woman, who'd gone into the back of the wagon with the shotgun, poked her head out and called to Nate.

"What's she want, Nate?"

"For you to bring your dog inside to her and for me to get her some milkweed."

Parker lowered the tail gate of his wagon, got inside, and lifted out the limp J.E.B. Stuart. He carried him up the steps that led into the medicine wagon.

"There, *chico*," ordered the woman, showing him a bunk on which to put the dog.

Parker had only a quick glimpse of the wagon's two bunks, many bundles, sacks, and boxes. It was sure all crowded up, he'd decided when she ordered him outside with a pointed finger and the one word, *"Vamos."*

Parker got down and went to stand by Hooraw to worry about J.E.B. Stuart. Nate had a lot more faith in Mexican witches than he did. He looked about him, wondering what direction he'd gone hunting for milkweed.

And then, from the east, he saw a fat man coming toward him, leading two sorrel horses. The white rooster trailed him, running.

The man came closer. Parker thought he looked quite surprised to see him, but then he smiled and said, "How do you do, young man. Where'd you pop up from?"

Parker Quiney looked him up and down in disbelief. His pants were sky-blue, his waistcoat black and silver, and on his long, ash-blond curly hair sat a high black silk hat. The pupils of his eyes were tiny black pinpricks on light green circles.

"Ya'd be Perfessor Tyree?" the boy asked.

"Indeed I would, young man, but you've not answered my question."

Parker kept up his lie. "I come from Fort Worth." Then he told the man of J.E.B. Stuart and the rattlesnake.

"Ah, I see. Well, fear not, lad, my good wife will heal the animal."

"I sure hope she can."

The professor nodded calmly. "She can do it. Rest easy on that score, my goodly youth." He tied the horses to a nearby small tree. "You haven't told me yet what brings you all the way from Fort Worth to these wild parts."

Parker sighed and told him of his errand. It looked as if he'd have to explain it to everybody in Texas sooner or later. This time, though, his questioner didn't bother to get up and look into the wagon back.

The professor only shook his head ruefully, took out a cheroot, and lit it. "A sad mission, indeed, for one of such tender years."

Then Parker asked, "What're occult sciences? What's a elixir?"

The man smiled again. "Magic, the courses of the heavenly bodies, seeing into the future, to reply to question number one. As for the elixir, 'tis a secret remedy of the Seminole Indians given to me by a great chief and medicine man many years past. It heals all ailments that afflict the carcass."

67

"Is the Mexican lady gonna use it on my dog?"

Professor Tyree laughed heartily. "The magic elixir is for human beings, boy!" He walked about the Quiney wagon, examining it, then opened the mouths of Pilgrim and Hooraw, looking at the length of their teeth. "Good strong team you have here, my lad," he stated. Finally he looked into the wagon. "You've got plenty of room left back there."

"What for?" asked the boy.

"To carry goods for me." The man slapped Pilgrim on the flank. "We're off in the morning, also traveling north. Why not come along with us? We'll keep that coffin of yours in our wagon naturally, since we can conceal it better there. It's hardly the sort of thing that would give my elixir customers a lot of confidence."

Parker was uneasy. "I don' know about that," he said stiffly.

The man leaned against the wagon, smoking. "How are you going to pay my lovely wife when she cures your dog?"

"I got some cash money with me, Perfessor." Parker gave the man a hard look. Nobody from Cottonwood or Tucker Springs would ask somebody for money for helping out anybody who'd been snakebit.

"Do you have twenty dollars, boy?" asked the man. "That's her customary fee."

"Nope. I ain't got that much."

"Well, you can work it out, can't you? Help Madame

Maria and me, and we'll help you!" Then he asked, "Are you running away from somebody?"

Parker glanced at the medicine wagon, hidden in a brake, as he'd hidden his that morning. It appeared to him that the perfessor didn't much want to be seen neither, so he decided to tell part of the truth. "I guess we could work it out. Yep, there's a gospel-shark preacher chasin' us who wants to put us in a orphans' home."

"Us?" The man jumped on the word.

"Ulysses S. Johnson and me, Sam Houston Smith."

"Where's this Ulysses? How old is he?"

"My age, I reckon. He's out scoutin' around after milkweed for yer wife. I jes' hope he knows what it looks like."

The professor stepped forward. "I'm glad to hear there's two of you strapping sons of Texas. And I'm glad you're going to travel along with us. Now I only have to ask you one more question before I start the fire for a good hot supper."

"What'd it be?"

"Boy, can you swim?"

Parker Quiney's eyes bulged. *Swim!* "Sort of," he answered, when he'd found his breath. "I do it better on the back of a horse, though."

"Well, perhaps your friend Ulysses can also swim. I do not require great artistic prowess, you understand, and I am perfectly aware that it is by no means an art commonly found in Texas. You need not tell me, lad, that Texas-spawned frogs can drown in mud puddles. I presume that was on the tip of your tongue." With these words the professor walked away toward the red wagon, leaving Parker staring after him. That was exactly what he'd been thinking!

Parker was still gawking after him when Nate came out of the brush, scratched and perspiring, but with a bunch of limp weeds in his hand. "Can you swim, Nate?" Parker asked him.

"Swim? What's wrong with you, Parker?"

Parker chuckled. Yep, you could knock Nate's eyes off with a board they bugged out so. "Don' call me Parker here. I'm Sam Houston Smith agin and yer Ulysses." The boy pointed to the professor kneeling near the wagon, starting a fire. "That's who I told him we are. That there's Perfessor Tyree. The Mexican witch's his wife." Parker sighed. "We're gonna be travelin' with them fer a spell."

"Why?"

Parker told Nate of the high fee to cure J.E.B. Stuart. "If my dog dies, we're lightin' outa here fast. I ain't so sure I wanta find out why that perfessor has it in mind for us to swim. He spooks me, and so does—"

He would have gone on about the Mexican witch, but the doorway of the medicine show wagon was flung open at that moment, and Madame Maria appeared on the top step. *"Niño,"* she cried to Nate and beckoned. *"Aquí. Pronto!"*

"She says, 'Boy, get here—fast!' " explained Nate Graber, as he ran toward her with the milkweed.

Parker and Nate never did learn what the woman did with the weed, but there wasn't one single yelp out of J.E.B. Stuart. After a big supper of chili beans and tortillas, Parker was permitted to see his dog. He lay stretched out on a bunk, bandaged, rolling his eyes up at Parker. When Parker called him by name, he wagged his tail.

The woman stood behind the boy, looking down at the animal, too. *"Si,* he will live. He will again run— and soon. We will go in the morning, my husband, me, and El Pollo, and you will go, too, eh?"

"Who'd that be—El Pollo?"

"My chicken. With heem I work."

Astonished, Parker Quiney left the wagon for his own and his bedroll. Whoever heard of anybody working with chickens!

It didn't seem to Parker Quiney that the Tyrees were in much of a hurry to get wherever they were going the next morning. Following wagon ruts, they traveled slowly northeast through unfamiliar country, spring green with grass. Each night when they camped, Parker and Nate went together to the medicine wagon to look in on J.E.B. Stuart. The fourth night the dog was sitting up when they entered.

"He's startin' to look natcheral agin," was Parker's comment.

"Si," she told him. "He's no more sick. Take heem."

71

As Parker went out with the slow-moving dog, Nate spoke to the woman in Spanish. Later Parker asked, "What were ya jawin' with the witch about?"

"I asked her when we were going to swim. She says tomorrow, *mañana*."

Parker looked out over the prairie. "There ain't one drop a water that I can see! She's sure gonna have to do some tall magic to come up with enough for us to do that in."

At noon the next day Madame Maria, who handled the sorrels, turned without warning off the road. Parker followed her with his team across the open prairie, then down into a wide gully. There the woman halted and called out, *"Muchachos,* bring buckets!"

"That's you and me, Parker," said Nate.

With the professor in the lead the boys walked down the gully, carrying buckets. At its end, to Parker's surprise, he saw a little blue lake.

The professor said, "Don't you bother with the dirty petroleum on the sides, my lads. Skin out of your duds, and swim out to the middle and bring me some of that good clean black stuff seeping up. Tread water. Get me some buckets of it."

Parker looked doubtfully at the lake as he got out of his boots. "We'll git oil all over us," he complained.

"This'll take care of that. My lovely wife makes it." The man pulled a cake of brown soap out of his pocket.

72

"It will outlather any soap in this land." Then he sat down on a rock.

By the time Parker was undressed, Nate was out swimming with his bucket. Parker entered the cold water slowly, the gravel hurting his feet. Floundering rather than swimming, he joined Nate, who was treading water near a black slick patch of water.

"How're we gonna do this?" he gasped.

Nate answered over the bucket rim, "We skim this off as fast as we can, I guess, then swim back."

For five minutes Parker tried to skim petroleum. It seemed to him he got lots more lake water than oil. "It ain't easy payin' for J.E.B. Stuart's doctorin'," he told Nate. "Yer turnin' blue. I reckon I am too. I'm goin' back before I git drowned out here. How about you?"

"I'm coming, too."

Pushing the buckets in front of them, the boys came slowly to shore. "This here's the best we can do, Perfessor," Parker Quiney said, panting.

The man got up and looked at the black-streaked water they'd brought. "It'll do fine, boys. I'll take these buckets back to the wagon."

"What's the petroleum for?" asked Nate.

The professor's eyebrows went up into buttonhook shapes. "Young man, it is the basic ingredient of the elixir! This very afternoon you shall aid Madame Maria and me compound the secret formula we'll sell in four days' time in Hunnicutt. Now wash yourselves and don your raiment. The soap reposes on the rock."

Parker looked at his oil-grimed arms and shoulders. "That soap'd better be good."

It was the all-fired latheringest stuff Parker'd ever seen, even if this creosote-stinking hunk didn't get the oil off too good. Because the soap didn't smell nice, Parker would have thrown it away, but Nate put it into his pocket. Nate was inclined to be a string saver, Parker already had learned.

"Ya don' swim so bad," Parker said to Nate, as they went back to the wagons.

"My pa taught me."

"It appears to me he taught you a heap of things."

"He did." Plump Nate trotted to keep up with Parker. "I could teach you Spanish or how to read and write, Parker."

"Not me. Tryin' to do that when I don' want ya to would be riskier'n braidin' a mule's tail, Graber. Give it up."

That afternoon was a busy one. Parker and Nate washed bottles for the elixir while Madame Maria stirred a great iron kettle of some brew. They didn't see what she put into it, but they sure smelled it.

"That stink would make a goat sick," Nate whispered to Parker, as she tossed in some mysterious-looking dried weeds she'd brought from her wagon.

When the bottles were washed, the professor set the boys to work with a funnel filling them a third full

74

with the petroleum and water. Then, while J.E.B. Stuart lay on the warm grass watching and El Pollo scratched around the Mexican woman's bright skirt, the professor brought out a wooden keg and commanded the boys to pour some of its contents into each bottle until it was two-thirds full.

Parker sniffed it first. "It's whiskey," he informed Nate. Then he fell silent as the professor came by with a tiny keg under his arm and from it measured out into each bottle a pinch and a half of black speckly powder. When he'd gone, Parker told Nate, "That was gunpowder!"

Last of all came the warm witch's brew, a thick black-red mass that stunk so high to heaven that Nate put his hand over his mouth, nauseated, and J.E.B. Stuart headed under the Quiney wagon with his tail between his legs. Daringly, while the Tyrees weren't looking, Parker stuck his finger into the last bottle before Nate put in the cork. He licked it off with one swipe of his tongue.

"Holy Gatlins!" he exploded, his eyes bulging. "It tastes like redeye made outa red pepper and rattlesnake heads. It'd draw a blister on a rawhide boot!"

Nate held his breath as he started to paste on the gaudy red-and-gold labels the professor had given him. "Parker, it says here on the labels that this can cure anybody of anything."

"It could kill anybody *and* anythin'," corrected Parker. Noticing that El Pollo was near him, he stuck

75

out his finger, and the rooster leaped back in a fluster of feathers. "This here chicken knows it, too." Parker sat on his heels looking after the bird. "I still don' know what that rooster does but crow to keep him outa the fryin' pan."

In Hunnicut Parker learned the answer.

Dressed up in a green-velvet frock coat the professor got up onto the seat of his wagon and stood in front of a purple curtain. Parker watched him while he did some sleight-of-hand tricks with bandannas, swallowed some fire and then a sword, but when he got around to peddling the elixir, the boy left. He knew Madame Maria was telling fortunes in a tent nearby. She couldn't use the show wagon today, since her husband had shoved the buryin' box into it. Parker guessed folks wouldn' feel so happy sittin' on it to have their fortunes told.

He watched Madame Maria go into the tent with a fat lady wearing a big black bustle. She was the first of a long line of waiting people. Now Parker went behind the tent where there weren't any folks, got down on his hands and knees, lifted the canvas, and looked into the tent. He saw the Mexican woman's red skirt and her woven leather sandals. Then he heard her low voice.

To the fat lady she said, "Much you have suffered. You have been married twice, and you will marry again!"

"Marry again?" the Hunnicutt lady twittered. "Lord's sakes, who'd that be who'd want to marry me?"

"His name is in the cards. My white bird will tell you. Choose a card for the lady, El Pollo!"

Parker shoved more of himself into the tent. He saw the women seated on stools at a small lantern-lit table spread with playing cards. He watched El Pollo fly up onto the table, scratch out one of the cards, and peck at it. Madame Maria took it from the bird's beak while the fat lady held her breath at the wonder of it all. Then the Mexican woman crooned, "The man you will marry lives nearby. He has brown hair, brown eyes, and a brown beard."

"Oh, yes," said the fat woman. "I know lots of men here around Hunnicutt who fit that description."

Parker pulled out onto the grass. He found Nate in the crowd in front of a torch-lit lantern, listening to the professor's spiel. "That Mexican witch jes' told a fat lady she'd git hitched agin, Nate. The rooster picks out cards fer her. I think the bird's a faker and the witch is, too."

Nate shrugged. "She cured your dog, didn't she? He's just fine now. He's got all his strength back." He pointed to J.E.B. Stuart, tied to the Quiney wagon so he wouldn't run off. J.E.B. was very busy scratching fleas.

"Mebbe she done that. I dunno." Parker stuck out his lower lip. "I think we oughta git our coffin and light out alone in the mornin'."

"*Your* coffin," Nate corrected. "It isn't mine."

"Aw right, my box then." Parker looked hard at him. "Are you still comin' north with me?"

"I guess so." Nate looked around at the throng buying the professor's elixir. "I don't see anyone I know from Cottonwood, and Preacher Symonds isn't here, but I think I'd like to put more distance between me and them just the same, Parker."

When the people of Hunnicutt had gone away filled with dreams of rosy futures and their pockets and reticules stuffed with Seminole Elixir, Parker sought out the professor in the medicine wagon. "I come for my buryin' box yer settin' on."

The man looked up at the boy from counting fifty-cent pieces. "Why, lad, you don't need it. There's no call for you to be on your way so soon. We've only begun our profitable relationship. Take your time to Ruination." He handed two silver pieces to Parker.

The boy took the money, and said, "Ulysses and me will be leavin' tomorrer."

"But, lad, I need more basic ingredients for the elixir. I sold all but four bottles here tonight."

Parker shook his head. "There're other folks in Texas who can swim. I got me a errand to do."

Tyree smiled and reached into his sleeve. He brought out a little double-barrelled pocket derringer. "Boy, it is not difficult to read your mind. I figured you'd be after me about this minor matter. So I took the liberty earlier tonight of putting some of the contents of your wagon into ours. We shall return to our little lake, replenish our stock of petroleum, and then you may go on your merry way. Now I bid you a pleasant good night!" He waved the derringer, still grinning.

Parker Quiney backed out swiftly. He found Nate at the Quiney wagon, patting J.E.B. Stuart. "The perfessor's a flannelmouth liar. He ain't got no more heart than a banker has, Nate," Parker ranted on. "He's gonna work us some more swimmin' back at that there lake. He's stole our grub, too, and our Winchesters, I bet." The boy looked under the seat for the rifles and found them gone. "The Tyrees are as bad as them Symondses—even if the perfessor says he was in the Confed'rate Army."

'What are we going to do?" asked Nate.

"I dunno. Figger some way outa this mess, too." As he pulled his bedroll out of the wagon and threw it underneath, Parker added, "I don' think we better try burnin' down that wagon of the Tyrees' though. That'd burn up my coffin, too."

At sleepless midnight, J.E.B. Stuart crawled over into Parker's blankets. Parker petted him while he thought, and then he smelled a funny creosote smell. It made him sniff his dog. What'd J.E.B. been into? Some stinkweeds? Nope, the smell didn't come from him. Suddenly Parker knew. It was Madame Maria's brown soap in Nate's pocket. He smiled up at the wagon bottom, rolled over, and punched the boy next to him. "Hey, Nate, you awake?"

"No, Parker. I'm asleep."

Parker didn't pay any heed. "I done some fast fig-gerin' jes' now. This is what we're gonna do when them two are outa their wagon in the mornin'."

A little after sunup Parker and Nate had Hooraw and Pilgrim watered, fed, and hitched. Hungry them-selves, they waited impatiently with a bucket of water nearby. Nate had J.E.B. collared and in hand.

At last the red door of the medicine show wagon opened. Out came the professor to stretch and yawn in the spring morning. El Pollo hopped out behind him.

"Barin' his brisket to the mornin' breeze jes' like he ain't guilty as all git out," said Parker bitterly. To Nate he whispered, "We're gonna wait, remember, till she comes out and he goes to look at the sorrels. Then we got to move fast and git it done right."

The boys waited until the man lit a cheroot and sauntered toward his team some distance away. Soon the woman came out, too, braiding her long hair and singing. They watched her while she crept under her wagon as she did most mornings to take firewood she'd gathered along the trail out of the rawhide wagon sling.

"*Now!*" said Parker. He grabbed his astounded dog and hauled his mouth open so Nate could pour water into it. Then Nate dragged Madame Maria's soap back and forth across J.E.B. Stuart's teeth. In seconds his mouth was a mass of snowy foam.

"That's enough!" ordered Parker. "Put the bucket back in the wagon."

Parker gave the very bewildered J.E.B. Stuart a push. "Go on, J.E.B.! Git that there chicken!" The dog was off in an instant after El Pollo. Around and around the medicine wagon they went, yapping and squawking.

"Mad dog! Mad dog!" the boys shouted together, sprinting for the red wagon while the Mexican woman cowered beneath it and the professor stood transfixed near his team, his cheroot shivering between his teeth.

Together Parker and Nate slid the coffin out of the wagon, ran with it to Parker's, and shoved it inside. While Parker climbed up to the seat, Nate made another trip to the Tyree wagon. He came out this time with the Winchesters, which he threw up to Parker, then ran back for the third time.

Parker, who'd seen J.E.B. Stuart and El Pollo heading north, drove to the Tyree wagon before Nate came out again. "Come on, Nate," he yelled. "Hurry it on up. We can't let nobody shoot old J.E.B. for a real mad dog while he's goin' through town."

Nate popped his head out, his eyes wild. "There's six gunnysacks in here, Parker. I don't know which is which—theirs or ours."

"Grab any three a 'em. It don't matter which."

Nate ducked back. An instant later he come out with three sacks and scrambled with them onto the seat next to Parker. Oblivious of the Tyrees, who were yelling now, Parker slapped his team stingingly on their rumps with the reins and shouted "Giddap, you horses!"

81

The team went from a trot to a canter in seconds, then into a gallop.

They reeled through Hunnicutt on J.E.B. Stuart's trail, avoiding other wagons and carriages, moving crazily every which way on the street. Teams were rearing in their traces. A driverless horse and carriage accompanied the boys for a time until a bellowing man ran out and stopped it. Ladies screeched. Horses at hitching posts pulled loose and raced up and down with town dogs chasing them. There was not one sight of J.E.B. Stuart—or El Pollo.

Skillfully dodging every moving thing, Parker called to Nate, "Some Hunnicutt folks stay up all night or git up early, don' they? I didn' reckon to see so many. I think old J.E.B.'s a half mile outa town by now."

Nate didn't reply. He was crouched down on the seat, holding his oversize hat with both hands to keep it from blowing off in the breeze they were making.

A mile out of Hunnicutt Parker began to whistle for his dog. For a while it seemed to him that J.E.B. Stuart wasn't going to come to his signal, or he'd never stopped running, but finally he limped out exhausted from under some brush. Parker reached for the water bucket, after shifting the reins to Nate, jumped down, and put his arms around the trembling dog's neck.

Tenderly he rinsed J.E.B. Stuart's mouth, then lifted him into the wagon. "You done some real fine runnin', J.E.B.," he told the animal. "I'm proud of ya. Rest yerself up now." Parker spoke to Nate, laughing, "I bet we sure made that witch and perfessor mad as wet hens 'cause we got away."

Nate was laughing, too. He held up a bottle he'd taken out of one of the gunnysacks. "They'll be madder than that, Parker. We've got Professor Tyree's last four bottles of Seminole Elixir."

"But what about our grub, Nate?"

The plump boy frowned. "I left most of it behind, I guess. I certainly got the wrong sack here. We're getting low, Parker. We've only got about enough to last us for a week."

Parker got up onto the seat and took the reins again. "That much oughta take us to Buffalo Notch. We'll git ourselves some more grub there."

"How far is Buffalo Notch?" asked Nate, putting the elixir back.

"I asked a cowboy I met last night watchin' the perfesser eatin' a sword about towns to the northeast a here. It's eighty miles, he says."

Nate was satisfied.

"It's on the way to Whiskey Creek." Parker drove a hundred yards and added, "We ain't hookin' up with no more folks along the way."

Nate Graber looked over his shoulder at the already-asleep J.E.B. Stuart and nodded agreement. "Yes, I think maybe I've seen enough of Texas hospitality for a time, too." His voice sounded worried. "Parker, Madame Maria certainly cursed us up one side and down the other when we were leaving."

Parker snorted, "I bet she could cuss good enough in Spanish to grow hair on a comb."

Nate told him glumly, "Oh, it wasn't swearing. She said she wished the Comanche Indians would get us and scalp us. She put a real witch's curse on us." He looked at Parker. "That's Comanche country we're going to near Ruination, isn't it? Madame Maria told me it was a couple days back. Mexicans hate Comanches, Parker!"

Parker Quiney was frowning. "Hearin' she cussed us like that makes me wish we'd grabbed her old El Pollo and hogtied him for our skillet when we busted loose. That woulda served her right!"

4
Blood
Feud

Parker shot a rabbit on the second day out from Hunnicutt, and that night Nate proved his true worth as a cook frying parts of it.

Lying back on his elbows on his bedroll, Parker said over the yelping of coyotes, "I allow old Nerissa couldn' do no better with a skillet."

"You haven't talked much about her," Nate remarked.

"There ain't much to talk about. My brother upped and married her without no 'by your leave' to me or my little brother or the weaner gals."

"Well, that was his right, wasn't it, Parker?"

"That ain't how us Quineys down home see it."

Nate was silent, then asked, "Parker, did Nerissa ever meet your brother, Jesse?"

Parker stared up into the twilight sky. A black hawk was circling high overhead. Seeing it made him think of Earl and Leo and the weaners, and he allowed he was homesick. Earl always said it was Parker's job to shoot hawks that came around after the chickens. "Naw, she never knew Jesse. He left home a long time back. He couldn' read or write neither, so we didn' git no letters from him—only that one letter somebody else wrote."

Nate shook his head sadly. "That's too bad, Parker." He sat back on his heels sopping molasses out of the frying pan with a biscuit for a while, then asked, "Why did all of your older brothers and sisters leave home as soon as they could? Was Earl cruel to you?"

Parker put his arms behind his head. "He was danged positive with us, but he wasn' mean. We got out fast as we could, so Earl'd have one less mouth to feed." The boy let J.E.B. Stuart lick his face, then pushed him away laughing and pulled his hat over his eyes. "I was gonna start travelin' Texas as a rough-string rider pretty soon."

Nate put down the skillet. "I hope you get to be one." He added thoughtfully, "And I hope to get to be a teacher someday."

"You're smart, Nate, for a damyankee," Parker

86

Quiney admitted. "You'll be a wisdom bringer aw right."

"I wish you'd quit calling me a Yankee. I don' call you a Reb, do I?"

"I don' care what ya call me, Ulysses S. Johnson. Long as I got to call ya that, I can't ever forgit ya are a Yankee, can I?" He drowned out the other boy's protest by bawling out a song. "All day long on the prairie I ride. Not even a dog to trot at my side. . . ."

For five days Parker and Nate journeyed north without seeing another human being. On the morning of the sixth day during a chilly drizzle they spied some men ahead moving around two covered wagons and an ox cart.

"You handle the team, Nate," Parker ordered. He gave him the slippery reins and reached under the seat for a Winchester.

"Who are they?" asked Nate, as water dripped off his hat onto his knees.

"I dunno, but they ain't got no women folk with 'em that I can see. That ain't a good sign. You keep on drivin'."

Nate's hands trembled, Parker noticed, but he kept a firm rein on Pilgrim and Hooraw, who tossed their heads, nickering when a rider came toward them from the covered wagons. As a long-haired man approached, Parker cocked the rifle. "Let me do the talkin'," he told Nate.

The man pulled in his horse and held up his hand, "Howdy!"

"Howdy," was Parker's reply.

"Where ya headin'?" asked the man.

"North."

"Jes' a leetle button, ain't ya?" commented the stranger, riding closer.

"I'm big enough for what I got to do," said Parker Quiney, moving on the seat to face the newcomer, the rifle easy across his lap.

The rider kept his distance. "Hell, boy, I only meant ya'd be too much of a colt to have any tornado juice to sell us."

Parker nodded. "I ain't got no whiskey. Who'd ya be?"

"Jes' a bone hunter. This here used ter be good buff'lo country. Well, I'll git on back and tell the boys there ain't no redeye in yer wagon."

"We've got Seminole Elixir," Nate whispered to Parker.

"Forgit it, Nate."

Parker watched the man canter back to the others. These men were gathering up the bleached bones of dead buffalo to sell to fertilizer companies at railheads miles away. Contemptuously Parker put the Winchester under the seat again.

"Maybe he'd have bought the elixir, Parker," Nate said.

"Prob'ly would have, but I wouldn' sell to bone hunters. Earl says they're even lower'n buffalo hunters. If he hadn' seen my Winchester, we'd a lost our wagon and mebbe been pecosed."

"What's that?"

"Got killed and sliced open and rocks put in us and been dumped in a river."

"Glory be!" exclaimed Nate. "I guess there are worse things than Comanche Indians!"

"Nope, there ain't nothin' worse'n Comanches. We're gonna be in Buffalo Notch tomorrer. Ya can leave anytime ya want to, remember. Buffalo Notch's a far piece from Cottonwood and the Widow Bybee. Ya oughta to be safe there. You bellyache too much sometimes for me, Graber."

"I wasn't complaining. I was only making conversation, Parker. You certainly jump to conclusions fast."

"It sounded like whinin' to me, scrub."

"You are very unreasonable, Parker Quiney," Nate said. He plopped the reins back into Parker's hands, folded his arms, and sat looking sternly toward the north.

Lockville and Hunnicutt had been real towns in Parker's horseback opinion, but Buffalo Notch hadn't quite made it yet. Oh, it was handsome, all right, settin' near the gap between long flat, blue hills plumb bushy with pecan trees, mesquite, and dark little cedars everywhere, but it didn't measure up to much of a town. It had just three frame buildings—a hotel, a general store, and what Nate told him by reading the signboard for him was the Sweetwater Saloon. The rest of the place was sod-roof shanties, little log cabins, and tents. A number of big yellow-brown bricks and heaps of small cannon balls lay stacked across from the general store.

Nate pointed to the cannon balls. "What are they doing there, Parker?"

Parker thought he knew. "I bet they're left over from the war and come cheap now for buildin'. That's prob'ly gonna be the jailhouse a this here place. Earl said to me once that the first thing a new Texas town builds is a saloon and the next thing's a jailhouse. Cannon balls stuck in mortar and bricks make up a good jailhouse." He cocked an eye at Nate. "Nobody can burn his way out of one a them."

"Maybe some windbelly like you could have talked his way out of the Symondses!" Nate commented hotly, as Parker stopped the team before the general store.

Parker Quiney refused to argue. "You're our king-of-the-pots cook so far, so what do we have to get here?"

"Beans and molasses and cornmeal and coffee and sugar," Nate said sourly.

Parker commented, "You can sure line yer flue with chuck better'n anybody I ever saw." He leaped down and tied the reins to the hitching post. "Git on down. You got to help me git the grub."

As Nate climbed down, an old man came out onto the porch of the store trundling a barrel. He stared hard at Nate, then harder at Parker. "Would one a ya be named Quiney?" he asked all of a sudden.

The boys eyed one another in a shocked silence. Then Parker said, "Nope. Nobody here's named Quiney." He motioned toward Nate. "This here's Ulysses S. Johnson, and I'm Sam Houston Smith."

"Is that the truth?" exclaimed the old man, sitting on the barrel. "Well, I been lookin' for a couple weeks now for somebody redheaded by the name a Quiney to be comin' through here with a coffin." He looked down from the porch over the wagon side and spat into the street.

"We're jes' cartin' that up north for some friends, mister," lied Parker. "We never heard tell of no Quineys. We're only stoppin' here for a spell to buy some more grub. You want to sell us some?"

"Sure, kid. Come on along in." The storekeeper set the barrel upright and led the way inside.

Nate asked in a whisper as they entered, "You think it's the preacher here ahead of us or the Widow Bybee's men?"

"I don' see as how it could be, Nate," Parker hissed to him. "We ain't seen nobody pass us on the way, and the gospel shark didn't know my real name."

"But the sheriff in Lockville could have told him."

This thought stabbed Parker. "You hush up. I'll do the jawin'. I'll get us outa this."

The store was a small place, smelling of coffee beans, and it was dim after the bright spring sunlight of the street. Bolts of calico were piled on shelves above barrels of biscuits, beans, and other staples. Rifles and shotguns rested on racks near stacks of shovels and pickaxes. Parker allowed that this one was like most every store he'd ever seen.

"Me and Ulysses want five pounds a beans and a small jug a molasses and some cornmeal and what else?" he asked Nate.

"Three pounds of coffee and four of sugar," added the other boy.

"Only three pounds a sugar." Parker jerked his thumb toward Nate. "I got to cure him a his bad sweet tooth." While Nate looked glum, Parker asked the laughing storekeeper, "Why're ya lookin' fer somebody redheaded with the name a Quiney and a buryin' box?"

"Oh, I ain't lookin' for him myself," said the old man, reaching into a barrel of beans for his scoop. "It's them Petersons in town who been lookin' for him."

Petersons! Parker was confused for a moment while Nate stared at him questioningly. *Petersons!* Then Parker drew in his breath, remembering. It'd been somebody named Peterson who'd killed Jesse—Starr Peterson!

"They live around here—these here Petersons?" he asked the storekeeper as casually as he could.

"Naw, they got a cow ranch a hundred miles southeast a here. They come to town some weeks ago to wait for a Quiney to pass through."

Parker felt cold all over, but tried not to let his feelings show. "How much fer the grub?" he asked the storekeeper.

"Two dollars, five cents," said the man, who'd been reckoning it up as he filled the order.

Parker gave him the money. Then, grabbing the supply sacks, he headed outside. Nate came behind him. "What's wrong, Parker?" he asked on the porch. "You got white as a sheet back there. Are you sick?"

"I got trouble." Quickly Parker told Nate of Starr Peterson. "If Petersons are lookin' fer Quineys, because Jess killed Starr, it means a blood feud!"

"What'll we do, Parker?" Nate was white-faced, too. "Shall we get out of here fast as we can?"

Parker shook his head. "I think that old buzzard in there spotted me dead to rights fer a Quiney. If I go now, he'll tell on me, and they'll be after me somewheres outside a town where they can bushwhack me easy."

Nate pointed toward the bricks and cannon balls. "There'll be a sheriff here. You can go to him."

Parker bit his lip, thinking, then said, "Nope. This ain't Quiney country. It appears to me it's more Peterson country. Petersons live the closest to this town. The sheriff'd be likely on their side." He gave Nate a fierce look. "The only way I see it is I got to fight it out!"

"We'll fight it out, Parker," said Nate, after a moment's worried thought.

Parker smiled even if he was plenty worried. "You don' even know how to fire a Winchester."

"But I can hold one and nobody will know the difference, and I can use this." Nate pulled Professor Tyree's derringer out from under his jacket, astonishing Parker.

"Holy Snakes, where'd ya git that?"

"It was in the medicine wagon, too. It's got bullets in it."

Parker let out a very deep sigh. "You stole it, huh? I reckon you Yankees are pretty corrupt at heart, the way Nerissa says mules are." He shook his head despairingly. "Aw right, Graber, you scout this here town while I keep outa sight. I don' want no Petersons shooting me from a tent. When ya find out where them Petersons are holed up, come tell me."

"I'll do it, Parker." Nate put away the derringer and came to stand beside the wagon, while Parker untied the team and got up onto the seat. "You stole the lady blacksmith's hat," he accused.

Parker sighed again. "Ain't nobody ever told you that two wrongs don' make a right?"

For an hour Parker sat fidgeting on the wagon box under a live oak half a mile north of town, his rifle on his knees, his eyes fixed on the direction of Buffalo Notch. Then Nate came stumbling over the rippling grass to him.

"I found them. It was easy," he panted. "Two of them are at the hotel upstairs. They're taking naps, the clerk told me. The other one is at the Sweetwater Saloon right now."

"Naps?" exclaimed Parker. He took off his hat and scratched his head.

"I guess they didn't expect you today, Parker."

"I guess they didn'. That's good news." Parker tied Hooraw and Pilgrim to the live oak and J.E.B. Stuart to the wheel again. He handed a Winchester to Nate and took his up again. "This here one of yours is loaded, too, and I got extry cartridges in my pockets." He showed Nate how to cock the rifle, gave it back to him, and added, "Don' shoot less'n ya need to. Aim at where a man's the widest. And be danged sure ya don' shoot me!"

Walking as swiftly as he could, Parker led the way back to Buffalo Notch. His stride was longer than Nate's, but Nate kept up by running every other step. "Where are we going first?" he asked once between puffs.

"The saloon. We'll take on the one that's alone first. That's what Earl woulda done when he was a Texas Ranger." Parker stopped in his tracks suddenly. "Did ya see that old buzzard from the general store go to the saloon?"

"No, I didn't, but I suppose he could have while I was at the hotel or coming back here. He could have told that Peterson there was a Quiney in town, all right."

"Then we better go extry careful," said Parker. "This here's what I want you to do."

* * * * *

95

The Sweetwater Saloon, like the general store, had never known a coat of paint, and the swinging doors marked it clearly as a tarantula-juice parlor. Parker stepped up on to the porch and hissed back over his shoulder to Nate, "There ain't but two horses out here at the hitchin' post, so I don' reckon there's a whole gang waitin' inside fer me. I'm goin' on in. You know what to do."

His heart was right up behind his teeth he was so scared, and his innards were churning so he thought he'd fall down, but Parker Quiney only hesitated for a few seconds. Then, his finger on the Winchester's trigger, ready to jerk the gun up and fire, he pushed through the doors. Once inside the boy stood still, looking wildly about him, aware through his fright of the raw lumber smell and the sharp tang of sawdust on the floor.

There were only two people in the whole place, a little man behind the long shining carved bar and a big white-haired one sitting alone at a table, a glass of beer in front of him. The other tables were empty. No one sat at the piano.

Words wouldn't come to the boy as he gawked at the man with the beer. Was he a Peterson? Well, he had a gun all right, one at his hip. But he wasn't reaching for it. This man sure didn't look to Parker Quiney to be gunnin' for anybody.

The bartender broke the silence the second after Nate, who'd been outside counting to five as he'd been

ordered, burst in after Parker with his rifle. "You brats,
rattle your hocks outa here. I don't serve no kids!"

Parker shook his head. "I'm Quiney! I'm lookin' for
somebody by the name of Peterson." He lifted the rifle
slightly.

The white-haired man rose to his feet, staring.
"That'd be me, Alf Peterson." He nodded; then to the
boy's great surprise, he smiled. "Are you a Quiney from
Santa Rosa County?"

"Yep." Parker waited, the Winchester ready while
Nate breathed hard behind him.

"I'm real glad to see you got here, boy," Mr. Peterson
said, moving out from behind the table, his hand outstretched. "How was your trip?"

Parker didn't answer him. He was too busy lookin'
where Mr. Peterson's gun was—on his left hip. That
was where a left-handed man would carry a gun, and
it was the right hand the foxy old longhorn was
stickin' out for him to shake. Nope! No Quiney worth
his salt'd ever fall for a trick like that, gettin' his right
hand caught and held and bein' shot easy with the left.

But Peterson brought his left hand forward, too,
away from his hogleg, and Parker breathed easier. Still
he was wary. The man went on, "I'm Starr's pa. I been
up to Whiskey Creek to fetch back my boy already.
I'm sure sorry about this. Jesse was your brother,
wasn't he?"

Parker stared into Peterson's eyes. Earl said you
could always tell a man was goin' to kill you by the

97

mean way his eyes looked just before he done it. This man's eyes weren't mean. They were mournful.

The boy let the Winchester down. So did Nate. Then Parker said, "Yep, Jesse was. Howdy." It didn't seem to him that Mr. Peterson had it in mind to shoot Quineys, so he let his hand be shaken. "I hear tell there's two more a you Petersons here in Buffalo Notch right now."

"How'd you find that out, boy?" The man sounded surprised.

Parker turned toward Nate. "This here's sort of a pardner of mine. He asked around town."

The big man nodded. "Yes, my wife and daughter are at the hotel asleep. This whole terrible business about Starr has been very hard on them."

"Womenfolk over at the hotel?" Parker gave Nate a mean look. Nate certainly hadn't asked the hotel clerk the right questions.

"Yes, boy. What's your first name?"

"Parker. This here's Nate Graber."

"And you're on your way to Whiskey Creek, too?"

Parker said, "Yep." He stepped back. "Nice meetin' ya, Mister Peterson. We'll be gettin' along now."

"No! No! We've been waiting for you. We wanted to meet some other Quineys. We sure took to Jesse."

Parker was astonished. "You *knowed* Jesse?"

"Sure. He worked for me a year until he and Starr headed farther north together for Ruination."

"Jesse and Starr was *friends?* I didn't know that."
Parker was so shattered he started to let the Winchester
fall onto the saloon floor.

"Good friends." Peterson caught the rifle before it
fell. He made a sour face as he returned it to Parker.
"I sure don't like seeing kids or most other folks carrying guns."

"Holy Gatlins, why'd they kill each other if they was
friends?" exploded the boy.

A look of deep sadness came over Mr. Peterson's
broad red face and tears came into his eyes. "I don't
know, Parker. I thought maybe you would. That's one
of the reasons we've been waiting here in Buffalo
Notch." He gazed into the boy's bewildered face, then
said, "Come on, boys, sit down with me and have something to wet your whistles." He called to the bartender
over his shoulder, "What've you got for the kids here?"

"Sarsaparilla and cold tea, that's all," said the man
behind the bar. "The sheriff don' like me havin' weaners
in here."

"We are not weaners," snapped Nate to Parker's
amazement. He'd never heard him talk like that before.

Peterson laughed and told the bartender, "I'll vouch
for these boys to the sheriff if he comes in. Bring 'em
some tea and boiled eggs."

Parker took a chair at Peterson's table. Then Nate,
who stared his full at the splendors of his second Texas
saloon, did too.

As the bartender set a bowl of eggs before them, Mr. Peterson asked, "Parker, did a rider bring you Quineys a letter from Mr. O'Hearne?"

"Yep, that's how my brother Earl found out about Jess bein' killed."

"I thought so, and I figured a Quiney would be going to Whiskey Creek to bring Jesse home. Have you got the letter with you, son? Could I compare it with mine?"

Parker shook his head. "No, sir, I ain't." He decided this old longhorn Peterson meant him no harm, so he leaned the Winchester against the table. Nate placed his rifle next to Parker's.

"We buried Starr in our family graveyard last month," said Peterson. It was his turn to shake his head. "You're pretty young to be goin' on this kind of errand, ain't you?"

"Parker's the oldest Quiney at home—next to Earl, his biggest brother," explained Nate.

"You hush up, Nate. I'm doin' the talkin' here on Quiney bus'ness," said Parker. "Folks keep tellin' us we're only fryin' size, but all the same we're goin'. You gonna try and stop us?" He half rose from his chair.

Peterson shook his head. "Got a short fuse, haven't you? Well, that was like Jesse and Starr. Starr was a redhead, too. I guess you don't know that, do you? No, I'm not going to try to stop you. It's what Starr would have done when he was your age." The man looked bewildered and shook his head. "But I still can't figure out why those two boys killed each other."

Parker sank back into his chair. "Didn't you see nobody up there on Whiskey Creek to ask?"

"I saw this here O'Hearne and two cowboys of his. There was another one who was supposed to have talked with Jesse just before he died, but he was away somewheres all the time I was there. Nobody could tell me anything much, boys. All I brought home to tell Mother was that guns did it. She never did take to Starr's carrying one—even if Texas menfolks generally do."

Suddenly the man slapped the table with his palm, startling Parker and Nate, who sat deep in gloom, listening to him. "Colts, I want to buy you two the biggest steaks the hotel's got for supper tonight. You have to meet my wife and daughter."

The boys looked at one another. Parker caught the half shake of Nate's head and saw his warning eyes.

"Aw right," Parker said firmly, "but we ain't stayin' overnight in no rooms. My wagon's out on the prairie, and so's my dog waitin'. Nate'll stay here with ya while I go out and fetch 'em in to town."

As Parker downed his cold tea, Peterson wanted to know, "Why did you leave your wagon out there?"

"Because we thought you was lookin' to feud with the Quineys. The storekeeper told me Petersons were huntin' for Quineys."

To Parker's pleasure Mr. Peterson didn't laugh and make him feel like a fool. "I guess it could sure have looked that way, couldn't it? Feuds have started in

Texas over a whole lot less." He turned to Nate. "Have another boiled egg, boy. You've only gobbled five and you got that other leg to fill up."

Mrs. Peterson and her grown-up daughter looked alike, with strawberry-blond hair and mournful brown eyes. They didn't eat at all while the boys shoveled in steak and beans, but dabbed their eyes with handkerchiefs, watching them.

"They're such little boys, Alfred," Parker heard the woman whisper once to her husband. "The Quiney child's so much like Jesse and Starr. And they've got guns! You ought to stop them."

"He can't. I'm a hog for duty, ma'am," Parker told her. That stopped her from bawling and her daughter, too, though they kept on staring out of watering eyes.

As Parker got down that night to unhitch the team, Nate told him, "While you were saying good-bye to her father and mother and telling them about your being a hog for duty, Miss Peterson said she'd pray every night that the terrible Comanches wouldn't get us. She says her father heard there were some roaming around up near Ruination!"

Parker only grunted as he reached for the leather hobbles he kept in the wagon to put on Pilgrim and Hooraw so they could graze nights. Let that old coyote out on the prairie wailin' his head off answer Graber. Danged if he would!

5
Lily
Bass

There was no wagon road north from Buffalo Notch—
only the trail the hooves of cattle had made when they
were driven to market. Each night that the boys camped
Parker waited for the North Star to rise and pointed
the wagon tongue at it so he would know which way
to head in the morning.

"It's like navigating at sea," said Nate the first time
he saw Parker do it.

"I dunno about that. It's what Earl told me to do so
I wouldn't ever git lost when there's nothin' like a hill.

We're goin' north and west now. That's the way Mr. Peterson told me to travel. I can tell west 'cause it's on my left hand where the sun goes down. The next place we git to is Merrick."

"I sure wish you could read," sighed Nate. "You think like an Indian."

"All you know comes outa books, you scrub," said Parker Quiney sourly.

The tall grass north of Buffalo Notch was spotted all over with yellow black-eyed flowers and pink primroses. The thick green grass was fine for cow brutes, Parker allowed, but its thickness made him worry. There must have been a lot of rain lately in this part of the country. Rain means that the streams could turn out to be hard to cross. Several times before they reached Merrick, forty miles from Buffalo Notch, they went cross-country out of their way to find shallow safe fords. Not unless he was forced to did Parker plan to swim the team or go to the work of cutting down trees to float the wagon across—not with "greener" Graber along. Nope, he wasn't fit to ride a river with. With another Quiney, even little Leo, it woulda been different.

Parker allowed it was a big relief to him the morning he spied a tent town ahead of him on the prairie. "That'd be Merrick, I reckon," he told Nate.

"Merrick seems to have only one real house. That would be the saloon, I suppose?" was Nate's question.

Then he added, "Merrick must be newer even than Buffalo Notch."

"It appears that way, don' it?" At that moment Parker heard some noise. "Hey, what's that?"

"It's music! It's women singing and bells, too!" said Nate.

"Out here on the prairie?" exclaimed Parker.

A surrey came rolling toward them out of the grove of trees over thousands of bluebonnets in bloom. It was a handsome one, sporting a dark-red top with gold fringe. A woman was handling the little black mare that pulled it. Bells on the mare's harness were jingling. Three other women sat inside, singing "Lorena." All wore bonnets with feathers and bright-colored, shiny-cloth dresses instead of calico.

J.E.B. Stuart heard the women, too. Barking, he jumped down from the wagon seat, where Nate had been holding onto him, and ran toward them.

"Here, doggie. Here, doggie!" called a high voice.

To Parker's embarrassment J.E.B. Stuart obeyed the call. He leaped up into the halted surrey and onto the lap of a woman wearing a bright blue gown with some sort of feathers around the neck.

"Fool dog!" complained Parker under his breath. "I'll go git him. This is what comes a Nerissa's hand feedin' him." The boy turned his team toward the surrey.

Now he saw the women more clearly. Three were good-lookers, but the fourth one was as handsome as a thirty-dollar pony. She had black hair, white skin, big dark eyes, and a tilting-up nose. She wasn' painted up half so much as the other three neither. It was her lap his dog was on, being patted and fussed over.

"They're saloon ladies!" whispered Nate.

"That sounds jes' like somethin' the Widow Bybee'd say," Parker hissed fiercely. "They're women folks. Ya oughta be polite to calico." He whipped off his hat, scowling at Nate, who now took his off, too.

"Mornin', ma'am," Parker Quiney said to each woman in turn, ducking his head. "That there's my hound. Can I trouble ya fer the return of him?"

The woman handling the black mare giggled. "Ain't that redheaded little boy the darlingest thing you ever saw, girls? Who'd of thought we girls out takin' the air would meet such charmin' boys?"

"I fancy the golden-haired boy with the great blue eyes," said another, a lady in a red dress and bonnet. She leaned out of the surrey and asked, "What are you two boys doing out here?"

Both Parker and Nate had blushed at the compliments, but Nate found his tongue first. "We're on a mission up to Whiskey Creek."

"There's nothing much up there but cows!" said the driver woman.

"My brother Jesse used to be up there," said Parker.

"Then why don't he come on down here?" asked the smiling lady in the red dress.

"He can't, ma'am. He's dead. His friend shot him.

106

I'm goin' to fetch him back for proper buryin' at home."

The women were silent. The prettiest one lifted J.E.B. Stuart off her lap and put him down so he could jump to the ground. Then she said, "We're very sorry to hear of that mission of yours. That's quite a chore for boys your age, isn't it?"

Parker looked modest. "Not fer us Quineys, it ain't."

The prettiest lady let out a little scream. "Jess Quiney's dead?"

Parker jerked his head up and stared at her. "Yes'm." She'd fallen back against the lady in the red bonnet. "Who killed him?" demanded the one in red.

"Starr Peterson, ma'am."

The prettiest lady let out another scream, a louder one this time. *"Lily! Lily!"* cried two of the ladies while the driver swung the black mare around and headed for town.

Parker stared after them, dumbfounded. "Don't that beat all, though? What'd that mean?" he asked Nate, after he'd put his hat back on.

"It means to me that Lily, whoever she is, knew your brother and Starr Peterson, too." Nate looked after the surrey rocking its wild way toward Merrick. "Maybe she'd know what they quarrelled about up in Whiskey Creek."

"Mebbe she would. Let's go ask her." Parker clucked to the team to "Giddap" again.

"Lily Bass," the first man they saw on the one street

of Merrick told them, "works at the Quickshot Saloon. It's the town's only saloon. You can't miss it." He pointed to the two-storied wooden building with an outside stairway.

"Much obliged," murmured Parker. Then he headed the wagon toward the Quickshot Saloon. As he reined in the team, he said, "You stay here, Graber. I'll talk to this here Lily Bass and find out what she can tell me." He gave the reins to Nate, leaped down, and shouldered his way quickly through the double doors.

Parker Quiney hightailed it out as fast as he'd gone in, with a woman behind him, her hand raised to swat him. As Parker stumbled for the safety of the wagon and J.E.B. Stuart yelping in the mud beneath it, the woman cried, "You git out and stay outa my place. I ain't lettin' no little britches in here. And, in particular, I don' want no Quineys!"

Parker, from the ground, and Nate, up on the seat, gaped at the woman standing on the porch, her hands on her hips. She had purple-black frizzly hair with black ostrich plumes in it, a long painted face, and a short sparkly black dress.

Parker pulled off his hat. "I only wanta talk to Lily Bass, ma'am."

"No, you ain't." The woman pointed at Parker, her finger trembling. "You upset Lily once a ready today. Ain't you Quineys done enough here in Merrick?"

The boy shook his head, bewildered. "Ma'am, I don'

108

know what yer talkin' about. I only got here jes' this minute."

She stamped her foot. "I'm talkin' about Jesse Quiney, brick-top. You git on outa here."

"You know Jess?" asked Parker.

The woman rolled her eyes toward the sky. "Did I *know* your brother?" She pushed her way back inside, shaking her head.

"Goshamighty, who was that?" Parker breathed half to himself, half to a tall blue-eyed man beside him wearing leather brush-bustin' chaps.

"That was the Widow Culbertson," said the man, who'd seen and heard all. "She owns this here saloon."

"What's she got against Quineys?" demanded the boy.

"I dunno. I don' know any Quineys, son. Mebbe I'll ask her." And he, too, went inside, his large spurs rattling on the porch boards.

Parker looked to Nate next. "Looks to me like she knowed my brother!"

"It certainly does," Nate agreed, "and she doesn't want to know you."

"Well, I aim to talk to her or this Lily Bass all the same," vowed Parker. "Did you git a good look at the way that old lady was dolled up. It was like seein' a forty-dollar saddle on a ten-dollar horse."

Nate smiled. "She didn't resemble the Widow Bybee much. How are you going to see her?"

Parker had been examining the outside of the Quick-shot Saloon with great interest, and he pointed to the door at the top of the stairway. "You bring the team alongside. That's where I'm goin'." The boy headed for the steps and clumped up them. At the door he stopped, thought for a moment, then put up his fist to knock. But before he could get a chance to, the door was jerked open, and he found himself looking into the muzzle of a derringer. The Widow Culbertson held it.

"I told you to git," she said between her teeth. "I figgered you'd try my outside steps next."

Parker let out a helpless sigh, then lifted his hands. When she motioned with the gun, he began to back cautiously down the stairs. She came out onto the top step. Parker, watching her face, saw her glance flicker away to the ground.

He heard her draw in her breath, then say, "Is that your wagon down below here?"

"Yes'm."

"What's that in it?"

"A coffin, ma'am."

"What's a boy like you doin' with one a them?" she asked, lowering her derringer.

Because her manner had changed, Parker took off his hat again, being polite to calico. He answered, "I'm takin' it up after my brother, Jesse. I'm fetchin' him back home in it, ma'am."

"Jesse Quiney's dead?" she asked.

"Yes'm. Didn't Lily Bass or the other ladies tell ya?"

"No, they sure didn't. They all busted in here, with Lily cryin' her eyes out, and hustled upstairs. They ain't none a 'em been down since. All one of the gals said to me was that it was about Jesse Quiney again. And that was enough to rile me up. The gals piled in here only a couple minutes before you came pushin' in downstairs."

"What'd Jesse do to rile you, ma'am?"

"Busted my hundred-dollar crystal chandelier from Galveston—him and that there Starr Peterson shootin' at it one night."

"Starr's dead, too, ma'am," Parker informed her. "Mr. Peterson went up and got him a ready. He come through here, but I guess he didn't stop at your place."

The Widow Culbertson held the door wide open. "Come on in, colt. Starr shot my piano four times last time he was in here, but seein' as how they're both gone, I'll let bygones be bygones." As she closed the door behind Parker, she asked, "How'd they both get killed? Comanche Indians? A stampede maybe?"

"They shot each other."

"My God!" muttered the woman. "I always said there was more guns than sense in Texas." She dropped her little pearl-handled derringer into her reticule, sniffing. "Well, what can I do fer you, Quiney?"

"Do you know what my brother and Starr Peterson'd fight over?"

"Naw." Her black plumes fluttered as she shook her head. "They got along in here like love and kisses."

"Can I talk to Lily Bass then? Mebbe she knows."

"All right." The widow sighed. "I told that Lily she was playin' with fire lettin' both them cowboys spark her. When they left here, each one was thinkin' he was her sweetheart."

"Both of them?" Parker was shocked.

"Uh-huh," said the woman. "I'll go fetch her. Take a seat, kid." She went out another door, leaving Parker to look around the fanciest room he'd ever seen—all red and green plush, shiny dark wood, white marble tabletops, flowery carpets, and claw-foot tables. He didn't dare sit down on any of the elegant-looking chairs for fear of dirtying them, so he stood, listening to the ticking of a tall clock.

He waited a long time, then with the widow behind her, pretty dark-haired Lily Bass came in, red-eyed, a handkerchief to her mouth.

"Ma'am," said Parker, "I reckon you knowed my brother, Jesse?"

"Yes," sobbed the girl.

"Do you know what him and Starr Peterson was fightin' about?"

She fell onto a sofa, weeping. "I was dreadful to them, playing them off against each other." Suddenly she looked up at Parker. "Maybe they fought over who was going to be my true love. I gave each of them a lock of my hair before they rode out of town. Do you think they killed each other over me?" Her eyes held Parker fast.

112

He felt even his ears grow red with confusion. How in thunder was he supposed to answer that? If he said he didn't think so, he'd hurt her feelings, for sure. Earl said it wasn' much of a man who was ever mean to a lady. "Ma'am, I wouldn't be at all surprised if they done it over ya. Yer pretty as a painted wagon or a red heifer in a flower bed."

"Oh, no!" Lily Bass shrieked again, got up, and ran out, crying harder than ever, leaving Parker with the grim-faced saloon owner.

"I reckon I didn' say the right thing," he said to the widow.

She sighed, "You couldn' said a worse thing if you set your mind to it. I know Lily. She'll cry for a whole month feelin' guilty about them two cowboys. There's a trail herd comin' through, and I'll need her to jolly them cowboys along when they show up. Lily's my nightingale, my singer."

"Oh, I'm sure sorry," said Parker. "I don' know why Jess and Starr done it. I said what I said so Miss Bass wouldn' grieve."

The widow gave Parker a strange little smile. "Well, what's done is done. I did you a favor, boy. Now will you do me one?"

"If I can, ma'am." Parker thought of all the grown-up folks who'd recently asked favors of him and wondered what this one wanted.

"When you come back from where you're going, you'll probably be travelin' through Merrick agin. If you find out what them two was quarrelin' about, will you let me know what it was?"

"Sure. I'll come tell ya myself."

"*No!* Don't *you* come. Send that other kid with ya or somebody else with the word. I don't want Lily ever settin' eyes on you agin. If the fight wasn' over her, I'll be the one to tell her, and if you find out it was, I won' ever tell her."

His hand on the doorknob, Parker agreed. Then he asked, "She won' be lettin' two men spark her at the same time no more?"

"Not if they're friends," the widow promised. "I think Lily's learned her lesson." As Parker opened the door, the woman called out, "Hey, Quiney, are you hungry?"

He turned back at once. "Me and my pardner could eat some, I reckon."

"Well, you get on back downstairs. Hitch your team, and go to my kitchen door. I got the best Mexican cook in north Texas. She'll stuff ya both with chuck so hot with chili peppers it'll burn ya all the way to your toes and make your boots curl up."

Parker grinned. That'd suit him fine.

He and Nate stowed away a good meal of chili beans and meat-stuffed *empanadas* given them by a plump smiling Mexican woman. Then, while Nate was thanking her in Spanish, the saloonkeeper came into the kitchen with a man. He was the one Parker had seen earlier outside the Quickshot Saloon.

Lily Bass

"Are these here the two you had in mind, Ruby?" asked the man.

"Uh-huh. They're travelin' north like you are." The widow waved her hand toward the man. "Boys, this here's Harper Wicklow. He's trail boss a the herd comin' through town pretty soon."

"We didn' see no herd—jes' some stray cows," said Parker.

"My herd's comin' from the south and west of here," explained the man. He gazed thoughtfully at the boys. "Mrs. Culbertson's asked me to take you along with me and the herd."

"Are you going all the way to Whiskey Creek?" asked Nate hopefully.

"Not all the way. We cut off about a hundred miles west of it near a little place called Crawford. How's your team and wagon? Can ya keep up with us?"

"Yes sir, Mr. Wicklow," boasted Parker Quiney. "We won' be in yer way, and we'd be much obliged to travel with ya."

"Well, I'll take you, I reckon. You'll help the cook out. I travel some miles ahead a the herd. I'm here now for supplies."

"I know somethin' about trail drivin'. My brother Earl told me. He went up to Kansas once with a herd," Parker said proudly.

Wicklow nodded. "You kids camp north a town. We'll pick you up when the herd's going by." He turned to the woman. "Mrs. Culbertson, they don' seem too

115

big for their britches to me. If the redhead turns out to be like you say he is, old Keeler'll take it outa him fast."

The woman laughed. "I remember Keeler. Well, thank ya, Mr. Wicklow. It's a good deed you're doing for these here boys. The redhead's a leppie, and I reckon maybe the fat kid is too. The Good Book says we ought to look out for widows and orphans. Well, I gen'rally look out good for one widow I know—me, and I'm sure obliged to ya for helpin' me do somethin' for these pore leppies. I ain't forgot you told me in Abilene once you was a orphan too." Still talking, the Widow Culbertson led the trail boss out of the chili-smelling kitchen.

The moment they were gone Parker started to stuff his jacket pockets with leftover *sopaipilla* bread. "That jes' goes to prove we was wrong about some Texas folks, Nate. Look how good we got treated here in Merrick, and now we're gonna go north with a herd. Comanches won' git ya with them trail drivers along. Ya never can tell which way a pickle's gonna squirt, can ya?"

Nate asked the cook in Spanish for some of the puffy fried bread. He told Parker, "Take all you want. She says you're so skinny you have to stand up twice to make a shadow anyhow." Then Nate turned serious as he also put bread into his jacket pockets. "Parker, they aren't going all the way to Whiskey Creek with us."

"I heard the trail boss same as you did. We got a hundred miles to go on our lonesome."

"Yes, and all the way back to Cottonwood alone, Parker, with Comanches to worry about—and something else."

Parker saw how strangely Nate looked at him. "What somethin' else?"

"The something that'll be in the coffin behind us in the wagon then! That's what!"

6
The
Trail
Herd

"You don' have ta keep a goin' with me no more," said
Parker Quiney from the kitchen step, "but I'm goin'
ta Whiskey Creek or I'll bust a hamstring. Us Quineys
are—"

"Oh, I know," said Nate wearily, finishing the remark. "You Quineys are hogs for duty."

And he trailed the other boy out into the street.

The boys heard Wicklow's cows coming long before
they saw them. Hurriedly Parker ordered camp broken

and hitched the team himself, because he was more skillful at it, while Nate gathered up the skillet and doused the fire with water. They were ready on the wagon seat when Wicklow rode by at a gallop, waving his hat and calling out, "Move in behind the chuck-wagon, kids!" Over his shoulder he called again, "Get off the trail, redhead."

His cheeks flaming because he felt ignorant of trail herding, Parker took Hooraw and Pilgrim to a little knoll a distance from the worn track in the buffalo grass. He should have known better than to be in the way.

The noise of the hooves made a low rumbling, which grew ever louder. Prairie birds rose into the air. Jack-rabbits froze, then bounded away northwards to escape the herd of cattle.

"Where's Mr. Wicklow going?" asked Nate.

"To see what's on up ahead. He's lookin' for grass and water and a good beddin' ground for the cows."

Parker and Nate waited with J.E.B. Stuart between them on the seat as the point riders came trotting by a half hour later. They were brown-faced men in dark shirts, chaps, and corduroy vests. Neither gave the boys and wagon more than a flicker of a glance.

Behind them shambled the leader of the herd, a tall, brindle-splotched longhorn with a clapping bell around his neck. At his heels came more lead steers, some lowing as they were jostled by their companions, others tossing their wide, cruel horns from side to side. Dust rose from under their hooves as they destroyed the spring grass.

The left swing rider passed then, yelling, "Get along there, you cows," but the streaming herd showed no sign of coming to an end.

From the wagon seat, where he held fast to J.E.B. Stuart's collar, Nate said, awed, "How many are there anyhow, Parker?"

"Earl says a trail-herd boss lotsa times runs three thousan', four thousan' head up to Kansas." He looked out over the mass of longhorns. "Don' ya never git off anywhere's aroun' where one a them brush splitters can catch ya on foot, Graber. They'll hook a man if they can." Parker laughed, " 'Course, they'll go after a horse, too, if they git their dander up."

"You aren't scaring me, Parker Quiney," said Nate in what Parker had begun to think of as his wisdom-bringer voice.

Parker had decided by now that when Nate took on that way, there wasn't any cause to worry a subject anymore. He pointed at another cowboy passing and changed the subject. "That there'd be one a the flank riders. There's another one on the other side a the cows we can't see. They ride in pairs."

"When does the chuckwagon come?"

"Behind the drag riders. They're the las' ones. They follow up the cow brutes. The *remuda* and wrangler are behind the cook."

Still more longhorns poured by, stripebacks, brindles, red-and-white peppered ones, muleys, mealynoses, and blues. Finally, though, the boys heard shouting. As the last of the herd passed, two cowboys appeared out of the dust, bandannas over the lower part of their faces to let them breathe. One of them waved, and Parker waved back.

Soon the boys spotted the covered wagon approaching, drawn by four mules. Behind it trotted a large band of horses, the *remuda,* followed by a lone rider, the wrangler. Parker urged his team forward down onto the trail, which had been beaten to soft dirt by the thousands of hooves that had passed over it.

Nate said, "I guess that was the cook, Mr. Keeler, in the wagon."

"Yep, I reckon it was."

"Parker, he didn't stop for us. Maybe Mr. Wicklow didn't tell him about you and me."

"Mebbe not, but the trail boss asked us to come along. He's the number one man."

All that day the Quiney horses plodded along after the herd, always keeping the *remuda* and chuckwagon in sight. Once Nate asked hopefully, "Are chuckwagon cooks good, Parker?"

Parker grunted his reply. "Earl says some is and some ain't. He says they all make coffee black enough to melt down a horseshoe, though."

Late in the afternoon the wrangler, a yellow-headed boy about sixteen, dropped back and shouted to them,

"I'm Billy Lee. The coosie's jes' starting on up ahead to th' herd bedground. He says fer me to tell ya to git on up ahead of the herd, too. Yer gonna be old Keeler's helpers." The wrangler rode closer, grinning, and called out, "I'm glad it ain't me fer a spell. He's a ring-tailed whizzer on blue-painted wheels." Then he trotted back to his string of horses.

"What does that mean?" asked Nate.

"That the cook a this here outfit's a mean old cuss," said Parker, sounding glum. "The wrangler gen'rally does chores fer the king-of-the-pots. It appears to me he's mighty glad to be gettin' out from under it." Then he commanded, "Git a good grip on my dog, Nate, and hold on. We're goin' by them cow brutes. I don' want him gettin' trampled by no horned jackrabbits."

"All right," was Nate's grim reply, as Parker swung the team out onto the open prairie on the herd's right flank.

After a quarter mile at a trot he sent Hooraw and Pilgrim into a ground-covering gallop. Two hours of this pace with some rests for the horses brought them near a stream. There they found Coosie Keeler.

Just looking at the man made Parker swallow hard. Keeler wasn't big, but the look he turned on him and Nate as they brought the team in was a real shriveler. He stared at the boys from top to bottom out of little dark eyes, then spat a wad of tobacco onto the grass. Next he said, "So yer the leppies the boss told me was goin' with us fer a while?"

122

"Yep, I'm Quiney," said Parker.

"And I'm Jonathan Graber, Mr. Keeler."

The cook didn't nod. "Get on down. The skinny one'll unhitch my mules and stake 'em out ter graze. The fat one'll dig me my fire trench. Ye'll both pick up wood an' chips for the fire on the trail. Carry it in yer wagon, then put it in my cooney."

Inwardly Parker moaned. Picking up cow-dung chips wasn't his idea of a man's work. Well, while he drove the wagon Graber could do that job and dump them into the rawhide sling under the chuckwagon, too.

"We're taking a coffin up to Whiskey Creek," Nate volunteered as he got down.

"Do tell," came from Keeler, who'd pulled out a pipe and now stuffed it unlit into his tobacco-stained beard.

"We're going up there to get Parker's brother who got killed," Nate explained further.

The cook only grunted and began to fuss around the back of the chuckwagon, mumbling to himself.

"Come on over here, Nate," warned Parker, as he unhitched the chuckwagon mules, leaving his own tired team to wait. When Nate was next to him, he whispered, "Don' mess aroun' with cooks, Yankee, if ya don't want yer luck to run muddy. They're ornery as hell."

"I'll remember. Thank you, Parker."

That night was a busy one. The boys soon learned that Keeler was a hard taskmaster. While Nate dug the trench and started the fire, Parker peeled potatoes and filled the water barrels from a small nearby creek. He had no time to watch Nate at work or study the herd, which had grazed until sundown and now was being bedded down some distance away from camp. Keeler never gave him an idle moment. Finally, though, the cook judged everything to be ready—the beans, spuds, biscuits, beef, and black-as-the-devil coffee. Now the cowboys started drifting to the chuckwagon after Keeler sent out the word.

These strangers reminded Parker of Earl and the bronc snapper he'd missed seeing this time. They tied up their horses in silence and came to the wagon, taking up tin plates, forks, and knives. Every man gave him and Nate a slow nod or said, "Howdy" but nothing more until Wicklow, the trail boss, rode up, too.

"These leppies are goin' north a ways with us," he told the men. Then he said their first names and the boys', but Parker caught only Dallas, Red, and Billy Lee, the wrangler.

The men ate squatting on their high heels or sitting on the grass. Billy Lee had a wide grin for Parker, so he went over to eat with him, and Nate, without being asked, joined them.

"Where you come from?" asked the wrangler, after he reached out and gave J.E.B. Stuart a piece of meat.

"Santa Rosa County." Parker told him the truth.

The young cowboy shook his head. "I ain't never been there. I'm from Frio County."

124

"We haven't ever been there," said Nate.

One of the older cowboys who'd finished eating and dumped his plate into a big pot of soapy water came over, too. "I'd be Crockett Walters. I seen ya got a buryin' box with ya when I rode by yer wagon."

Parker explained his errand shortly to the little cowboy with the rattler-skin band on his hat. Crockett Walters listened politely, then took out a mouth organ from his vest pocket, shook a shower of tobacco crumbs out of it down on top of J.E.B. Stuart, and asked Parker, "You got yerself a hoss down there?"

"I got me a bay mare, by the name a Two Dollars. She's the fastest in the whole county," bragged Parker.

"How 'bout you?" the man asked Nate.

"I haven't got a horse. The people I lived with didn't have a carriage."

Billy Lee, the wrangler, hooted. "Well, they's ninety of 'em in a rope corral right near here, kid. Any time you wanta ride, lemme know."

"Thank you, I'd—"

Parker guessed Nate would go on for a long spell, and there was something he particularly wanted to know, so he interrupted. "Do you reckon anybody here woulda knowed my brother, Jesse, or his friend, Starr Peterson?"

Billy Lee's voice rang out over the camp, repeating the question, but no cowboy did anything but shake his head.

"Well, I jes' reckoned ya might have," said Parker.

"I knowed a Quiney oncet in the Confed'rate Army," called over the gray-haired cowboy, Dallas, helping himself to some canned peaches with his knife. "Amos Quiney was his handle. Any kin to ya, kid?"

"Naw, but my pa was in the Confed'rate Army."

"How 'bout yers?" asked Crockett Walters of Nate.

Before Nate could chew through the slippery peach he'd speared and get out a word without gagging, Parker answered for him. "Sure, Nate's pa was in the Confed'rate Army like everybody else here, I reckon. Did ya think I'd be travelin' with a damyankee?"

He looked around for approval, while Nate glowered and swallowed, and saw that the trail boss and everyone else, even Keeler, was nodding agreement with him.

The very tall cowboy named Red said, "There's three things in the world I ain't got no use fer—a Kansas marshal, a yeller dog, an' a Republican damyankee."

Keeler added in a growl, "I wouldn' give a moldy biscuit to no Yankee if he was starvin'."

Parker watching, saw Nate's mouth open to complain, then saw his jaws shut with a snap. His eyes bored blue holes into Parker's, though.

"Come on," bawled Keeler at that moment. "Dump in yer plates an' the leppies'll wash 'em."

Parker got up without enthusiasm. That wasn' a man's work neither. His sleeves rolled up, he scrubbed the tin plates, though, and spoke over their clattering

126

to Nate, who was wiping them with a not-too-clean towel. "I bet the Widow Bybee learned ya how to do dishes real good, scrub."

"You go to the devil, Parker Quiney," came Nate's infuriated whisper. "You're a liar telling them I was a Rebel like you."

Parker Quiney hissed over the kettle. "Look here, scrub. We're bein' done a favor. Ain't ya got no sense at all? The preacher or nobody else'll git us here. You open yer mouth, and the coosie'll quit feedin' ya. Ya want that should happen?"

"All right, but I'm not staying much longer with you to take your insults, Parker Quiney. The first chance I get I'm going."

"Scrub, that suits me jes' dandy. Light out whenever ya feel like it."

Finished, Parker went back to the fire and the cowboys. A sullen Nate trailed him.

Parker heard Red's words, "Damned if that ole muley steer didn' go and chew up my best Navajo saddle blanket. He'd eat mos' anythin'. I heard tell he was the only one of a herd that stayed alive one bad winter that froze off both his ears and his tail. They never growed back agin."

"That musta been the same winter my pa froze hisself ter death when the wagon box turned over on him," came from Crocket Walters, who poured himself more petroleum-black coffee out of the huge pot.

"Mos' likely," agreed Red. "That was a bad year.

That summer I got blackthorn poisoned. So sick I near upped and died."

"I recollect it too," put in Dallas, folding his arms around his knees. "It was a real bad year. I got hitched then to a female in Laredo who could talk the hide off a cow."

No one laughed but Billy Lee, who began to play "There's One More River to Cross" on his harmonica, then pulled out a knife. "Red, ya wanta play mumble peg?" he asked. "Ya got time before the next watch?"

Wicklow spoke for him. "No, he ain't. He's goin' now."

Red got up, followed by Crockett Walters, and headed for the *remuda* and fresh mounts.

"I can play it," volunteered Parker, stepping over Nate's legs to go to the wrangler. As he passed, he stopped and said. "Graber, yer swellin' up like a carbuncle yer so mad."

"Oh, be quiet," muttered Nate.

For a while it was silent except for the soft lowing bellows of a cow and coyote night sounds. Then Nate asked the trail boss, "Are there lots of Comanche Indians around here, sir?"

"There ain't supposed to be. I used to have to give 'em some steers six years back to cross their territory. They're supposed to be on reservations now, but I hear tell some a the young ones slipped their tether a while back and are ridin' around in bands."

The cook broke in, "They're madder'n roosters

caught in a rainstorm, too, because so many buff'lo got killed off by white hunters las' year. Them Indians set great store by buff'lo."

"It isn't right to kill their buffalo," Parker heard Nate say softly.

"Well, I can't see killin' off so many," agreed the trail boss, "even if they did git in the way of a herd sometimes. Fifteen years ago one a you kids coulda bespoke yerself a job with my outfit because a the buff'lo."

"What'd that be?" asked Parker, hauling Billy Lee's knife out of the sod.

"Takin' a rifle and ridin' ahead to scare the brutes out a the way." The man got up and stretched. "I'm fer turnin' in. We made twelve miles today. I wanta do as much tomorrer."

Parker watched him go to the chuckwagon, reach up on top of it, and pull down a bedroll. The boy returned Billy Lee's jackknife to him, rose, and strolled to his own wagon. Nate soon came after him with J.E.B. Stuart at his side.

"I want you to know something. I'm not speaking to you, Parker Quiney," he said.

"Suit yerself, scrub." Parker hauled out his bedroll and went back to the fire. Let the damyankee sleep under the wagon alone. He stopped in midstride, however, looked back and whistled for his dog. J.E.B was a Confed'rate dog. When the animal refused to come because Nate had begun to fondle his ears, Parker muttered some of the words Earl used on mules and went on to the fire.

"Where's that fat kid?" asked Dallas, while Parker helped him stomp over the ground to kill bugs that'd get into their bedrolls.

"Sleepin' with my pot hound."

"He talks kinda queer," remarked the cowboy, who spread out his bedroll, then took off his gun, boots, and hat, and crawled inside with them and his throwin' rope.

"Well, I took ta him once, but I don' think I'd do it agin." Parker began to haul at his boots. "But he's got some good points. He's purty smart, and he's gettin' more grit travelin' with me. If he goes all the way to Ruination, mebbe I'll make a man a him yet!"

Nate kept his vow of silence. Day followed day, and Parker Quiney learned cattle drivin' was a dull business and every day the same. Along around midnight the cows always stirred and changed the way they were sleepin', waking him up. Then he'd watch the stars and listen for a time to the singing of the cowboys on watch, soothing the animals back to sleep. Before long he'd hear old Keeler over him hollering, "You crawl outa there," and he had to get up to grind coffee and fetch water and help with breakfast. Next came Billy Lee with his string of wild-eyed mounts from the *remuda* and his call of "Hosses! Hosses!"

The rest of the day Parker followed behind the

drag riders, chuckwagon, and *remuda,* until Billy Lee dropped back to tell him it was time to follow Keeler. Then he'd whistle and wave for Nate, who was out foraging for chips on the prairie, to grab his bucket and come back to the wagon. Sometimes he wished Graber'd talk to him, even complain about doin' the dirty work gettin' cow chips while he sat like a king on the wagon seat, but there wasn't one peep outa him.

The only real joy Parker allowed he took in the drive was talkin' with Mr. Wicklow and his cowboys. Mostly they jawed about horses, but sometimes about pie suppers they'd gone to. Wicklow and Keeler and Crockett, Parker learned, could read. The others couldn't. But Billy Lee could use a rope better'n even Earl. Red was almos' as good a rider as the bronc snapper back home—even if rheumatiz hit him hard in cold weather.

A week passed, and Parker gave up trying to coax Nate into talking. He spent all his spare time with the cowboys now, showing how well he could ride any horse Billy Lee fetched him and how well he could do hooley-ann loops in the corral roping *remuda* horses. When the cowboys sometimes praised him, he always flashed a look at Nate, but Graber was never looking his way. He was busy shining up to Keeler.

One night the cook let Nate mix the sourdough for the biscuits. This time Parker saw Nate's glance of triumph his way and scowled back at him. Why be proud a that? It was woman's work!

131

Billy Lee was impressed, though. "I never seen old Keeler do that afore—trust anybody with the dough." The wrangler was sprawling on the ground, playing three-card monte with Dallas and Red.

"Mebbe the fat kid'll turn out ter be a coosie, too," said Dallas, pointing to the card on the right.

"Naw, he's gonna be a wisdom bringer," Parker scoffed, and waited expectantly for the cowboys to agree with him.

"They's lots worse things than bein' that," was Red's disappointing remark.

Dallas sounded sour. He'd guessed wrong on the card. "There's been plenty a times I wished I could read an' write. One time I got me a letter from a little old gal in San Antone. I throwed it away 'cause I was ashamed to have somebody read it fer me in case it was a love letter. Wish I'd growed up near ter a wisdom bringer and had me some schoolin'."

Parker Quiney had heard plenty. He got up angrily and went stiff-backed to see how Hooraw and Pilgrim fared. Staked out, they grazed peacefully. For a long time he stood looking south, thinking of Earl and Leo and the weaner gals. Yep, it sure was turning out to be a long way to Ruination.

When Parker crawled out of his bedroll the next dawn, he knew before the coosie told him that something wasn't right. It was May. That meant the days were getting warmer, but they shouldn't be getting this

132

warm or this damp. As he helped Nate and the cook with breakfast, he felt his shirt sticking to his back. There were black clouds coming up out of the southeast, too, darkening the sky.

While Parker sliced off bacon, he listened to Keeler and Mr. Wicklow discussing the weather. "Mebbe it'll blow over," said the cook. "I seen it like this before and nothin's happened."

"Well, we're goin' on anyhow," commented Wicklow, blowing on his coffee, "but if it don' look better before we camp, I'm sure gonna keep some more horses saddled up tonight." And then he rode off.

All that day Parker sat sweating on the wagon seat. He saw how red in the face Graber was as he brought in his buckets and dumped them into the wagon. J.E.B. Stuart's tongue hung out a country mile, and his sides heaved so bad Parker got out and hauled him up into the wagon, too. Parker almost asked Nate to get on up and "set a spell and rest," but didn't. He knew all he'd get was another sour look and a shake of Nate's head.

"Hog-headed scrub of a Yankee," muttered Parker to himself.

When Billy Lee came to them and waved northward as his signal for them to go, Parker kept his face straight ahead, not looking as Nate stumbled back to the wagon. All the same, one glance had shown him Graber's shirt was soakin' wet and his hair was plastered to his head.

As Parker drove past the herd, he noticed how the

longhorns bawled and jerked their heads. It was hotter now, and the dust choked him. Even through it he could smell some stink in the air. All at once he recognized it as sulphur, the yellow stuff Nerissa had spooned down him and other Quineys in March.

Parker found the country ahead of the herd strangely quiet. There wasn't a bird making a sound or a jackrabbit bouncing in sight anywhere—not even a breath of bad-smelling wind. J.E.B. Stuart trembled when he turned his head to look at him and whined. And it had got darker—lots darker than it should have been for that time of the day. The morning clouds hadn't ever gone away. They'd got thicker and blacker, and there were more of 'em.

Parker tried to catch his breath as he guided the team north. Breathing hurt him, and he guessed it hurt Nate, too. He heard him wheezing beside him. All at once a bright stabbing flash of lightning blinded Parker. He opened his mouth to say something to Nate about it, but sharp thunder drowned his words. The next moment J.E.B. let out a howl and jumped out of the wagon and tore off to the west.

"You come back here!" yelled Parker as more lightning blanked out the clouds. It was so dark the minute it was over he couldn't even see the dog. Still more lightning streaked hayfork patterns in the southeast. All at once he heard a rising roar.

"What's that?" cried Nate, pointing to Parker's head.

Parker thought he knew, because he could see the

fireballs running around the rim of Nate's hat. "Fox fire," he yelled.

"The wind's coming up, Parker," cried Nate, as the wagon started swaying each time a gust struck it.

"I jes' hope that's all there is!" Parker said under his breath. Then he slapped the reins and shouted to the team, "Giddap!" They began to rock across the bumpy prairie at a gallop.

"Where are we going?" cried Nate, holding tight.

Parker didn't answer. He looked behind him instead, and his face drained white. The roaring sound out of the south was stronger now than the wind from the southeast. He could see red flashes of fire. They meant only one thing to him—that the point riders out front were firing their guns into the ground. "The herd's runnin'," he screamed to Nate. "It's a stampede! They're tryin' to turn the lead cows with guns!"

"What'll we do?" In an eyeblink of lightning Parker saw Nate was salt-pork gray.

"Pray. And hang on!"

The Quiney horses raced ahead of the herd with Parker cursing and praying. For the first time he could ever remember the prayin' came easily. When Nate yelled into his ear, "Parker, I can see the blue fire on their horns," Parker tried to get more speed out of Hooraw and Pilgrim. Their manes flying, their nostrils dilated, the two raced on. But always the pounding hooves gained. Earl had always said there was nothin' faster'n a longhorn steer when it had a mind to run and had a scare throwed into it! The herd's rumbling thunder was so loud that Parker Quiney couldn't make Nate hear him. He could only keep the horses running.

In an instant the stampede was upon them, a point rider galloping by, his mouth open in an unheard bellow. Cattle surged up behind the Quiney wagon, saw it as an obstacle, split into two running streams of horns and hooves, and came together again ahead of it. Again and again longhorns slammed into the sides of the wagon.

Parker didn't spot the bump ahead of him because of the close-packed cattle. If he had, he couldn't have swerved to miss it. Hooraw and Pilgrim raced over it. The wagon rose for an instant in the air as the wheels hit it. Parker Quiney rose with it. As he did, he lost his balance on the seat and the reins were jerked from his hands. He clawed behind him for the seat, but missed it as another steer jostled the wagon.

Parker looked about him in panic. A great rolling-eyed brindle steer hurtled past him, fire gleaming on its long blue horns. At its heels pounded another, this time a stripeback. It ran so close alongside that Parker, who was on his hands and knees, could reach out and touch its hide. And then more terrified cows hit the wagon on Nate's side, throwing Parker forward. Another instant and he would fall down on top of the team's harness.

With a wild cry Parker leaped out of the moving wagon onto the stripeback steer. Clamping his knees around its barrel and his arms about its neck, he buried his face in its dust-smelling hide. He felt its hard knobby backbone under his cheek and chest and its muscles pumping as it ran.

"Oh, Lordy," he mumbled over its whistling breath as it started to rain huge drops. "I'll go to church ever' Sunday from now on if I ever get outa this."

The boy looked out only once at the maddened cattle running alongside him. Then he closed his eyes and hung on, praying. After a time when the stripeback had settled to a rolling gallop he dared inch along its rain-slicked back and grab hold of a horn.

Parker Quiney had no idea in the thunder and roar which direction the stripeback took him or how far. He clung to it, eyes closed from fright until he could hear only the sound of the wind. Then he opened the eye that wasn't jammed into the cow brute's hide. It had stopped raining. He and the stripeback were alone, though it was still running to beat hell, heading straight for a patch of mesquite. "Oh, Lordy!" Parker shut his eyes again, this time to save them from being scratched out.

He felt the stabbing pain of thorns cutting his arms, legs, and face. At last he let go his grasp and fell. "Go on, you brush jackrabbit," he whispered. "You keep on runnin'."

Freed from his weight, the stripeback rocketed off into the mesquite, leaving the boy on the ground. Parker lay there for a while, then he sat up. He looked down at his shirt, in rags now, and put his hand to his face. It came away bloody. But his boots were just fine, and even if he was shook all the way down to 'em he still had on his hat. "Holy Gatlins," he said softly, "I done it. I reckon it's somethin' Earl ain't never done neither. Mebbe no other Quiney ever did!"

After a while Parker got up and stared into the sky. The black clouds were passing to the west. The thunder was only a growling in the faraway distance. The storm was just about over. But suddenly he remembered something. His steer had bolted out of the herd. Other cows might have done that, too. Longhorns were plenty dangerous to a man on foot. Parker decided what he needed was a good safe place out of the brush, which could harbor snakes as well as cow brutes. Besides, he ought to have a look at where the stripeback had brought him.

He found a solitary tree on the edge of the mesquite and climbed up it. For a full minute he looked in every direction. Nothing! There wasn' nothing one bit familiar. And there wasn't no herd anywhere—only prairie and some cactus and wet bluebonnet flowers and puddles.

"We musta run miles," he told himself. He slumped in the tree. Yep, he reckoned he knew what Mr. Wicklow was thinking and the others, too—if they hadn' been killed. They'd think he'd, for sure, been trampled to death. Nate would have told 'em what'd happened —that he'd jumped aboard a steer. Mebbe Graber was

138

dead, too. Nate coulda slid out onto the ground after he'd jumped on the stripeback the next time some cows ran into the wagon.

Stinging tears started down Parker's cheeks. He'd never get to Whiskey Creek now. He'd prob'ly die out on the prairie, starvin' of thirst. Mud-puddle water didn't last long this time of the year, and he didn' have no canteen. A long time from now somebody passin' by mebbe would find his bones turned white by the sun.

Parker got down and drank from one of the puddles, then scooped water with his hands into his hat. He carried it with him back up the tree. There was no tellin' if the stripeback'd come out of the mesquite any minute. He'd spend the oncoming night in the tree.

Miserable in its crotch, his hat leaking onto his lap, Parker waited for the North Star to come out. He knew the herd would go north—if the cowboys could ever get them together again. He wondered if the trail boss would send somebody out lookin' for him when he'd got the cows milling around in a circle and settled down. Earl had said trail bosses sent out cowboys to make the gather of lost steers, but would they look for somebody who was probably dead?

When the North Star rose, the boy hauled off a boot and threw it on to the ground below the tree to mark the direction. He drank some bad-tasting water and thought of Nate. If that scrub of a Yankee had come through the stampede all right, he'd go back to Cotton-wood. He'd take the team and wagon and J.E.B. Stuart with him, too—if the dog hadn't got trampled. Parker sniffled and rubbed away his tears with his scratched hand. He hoped Graber'd go out to the ranch and tell Earl what'd happened. Earl would fancy the idea that Parker tried to ride a steer. He'd pass it on to the bronc snapper. Even if Earl knew it hadn't done no good, Earl'd think that took some grit.

At sunup Parker got down out of the tree, put on his boot, and started walking northeast. He knew he was west of where he'd been yesterday. He stumbled along for hours. Sometimes he sat on the ground to cuss out his boots. Once he said to a passing jackrabbit, "Aw right, I wish I had me Graber's sodbuster shoes right now."

That night, his stomach grumbling with hunger, Parker slept next to a good-sized spiny cactus. He recognized the plant as one you could get some water from, and he made himself feel better by chewing its thick stems. But he couldn't stay under that cactus forever. So once more he put out his boot to point to where the north was.

The next day he limped on 'til noon, then sat down sadly on the buffalo grass. The sun was gettin' mighty hot on his back, and there wasn't one speck of shade in sight. There wasn' anythin' to see but a bare purple-blue butte on his right. Parker put his head in his hands. He wasn' thinkin' of Whiskey Creek now or of Earl or the herd or anything but food. All he could see in his mind's eyes was a big plate of beans and biscuits.

When he heard a coyote yap loud enough to break into his dreams of Keeler's chuckwagon joys, he muttered, "Oh, hush up, you no-good excuse fer a dog." A ringing yelp in his ear and a rough tongue slobbering on his cheek made him lift his head, though. It wasn't a coyote at all. It was J.E.B. Stuart.

"Where'd you come from? You got out of the way in time before the cows got to ya, huh?" Parker reached out and grabbed the dog to him, burying his face in J.E.B.'s soft white mane.

But the dog wouldn't be held. Barking, he wriggled loose from Parker's arms and ran ahead. Painfully the boy got up. His feet were so blistered by his tight-fitting boots he could hardly stand. But he reeled after J.E.B. Stuart.

Within a couple of hours Parker saw a rider coming toward him over the endless grass. It was Mr. Wicklow. Wicklow didn't say anything, but reached down and pulled the exhausted boy up onto his horse and held him before him in the saddle.

"I'm kinda dry. . . ." Parker began.

But the trail boss said, "Don' talk. You'll be jes' fine in a little while."

Parker Quiney had no idea how far he and Wicklow rode with J.E.B. Stuart running along beside the horse. Dizzy with weariness, Parker saw the cook, the cowboys, and Billy Lee bending over him as Wicklow laid him on the grass. Then Nate's worried face came popping into view over the wrangler's head.

"You ain't dead neither, Nate?" croaked Parker.

"No, he isn't, but we all sure thought you was," the cook told Parker. "Everybody did but Nate there. He kept tellin' that pot hound to go out lookin' fer ya even when nobody could find hide or hair or bone of ya."

"My wagon an' my team?" asked Parker.

"They're all right. They kept up with the herd," came from Billy Lee, who gave Parker some water from the chuckwagon dipper.

Parker shook his head, trying to focus his eyes better to see Nate. "How come you didn't take 'em and light out on your own for someplace, Graber?"

"No, I was going on up to Whiskey Creek all the same."

"Without me along?" exclaimed Parker, rising up on his elbows.

"He surely was," said Keeler. "I never seen two such hogs for duty as you colts."

Later after Parker's cuts and blisters had been doctored by the cook with gosh-almighty mean horse liniment and lard and he'd been fed, Nate came to sit beside him, talking. It had taken all that first night to get the herd calmed down. The next day the cowboys who could be spared had spent hours searching gullies for strays while the herd halted on the trail. It had been pure blind luck that Mr. Wicklow had gone Parker's way on his last gather and heard J.E.B. Stuart barking his head off and spied Parker walking.

"Mr. Keeler says you'll be able to get your boots on again by the time we reach Crawford three days from now. We're starting out tomorrow." Nate added, grinning, "You certainly have some blisters there. I'll bet you wished plenty of times you had my shoes on."

"Mebbe once or twice," Parker admitted grudgingly.

Nate leaned over and asked softly, "Did you cry? I did."

Parker scoffed. "Naw." Not meeting Nate's eyes he sat up, wincing, as he braced himself on his flannel-wrapped feet. "I thought I was gonna do it once, though, Nate." Then Parker asked, "What did the cowboys and Mr. Wicklow and Keeler think about my ridin' a longhorn?"

"They wouldn't believe me when I told them at the beginning, Parker. They thought I was seeing things and that you really jumped onto one of the *remuda* horses. But I made them believe me after a while. Then they said it would take a Santa Rosa County featherhead even to try a fool thing like that and a bigger one to get away with it."

Parker shook his head, and asked, "You was really goin' up after Jess alone, Nate?"

Nate blushed. "Yes, I was."

Parker was too overwhelmed to say anything except, "I'd a been much obliged to ya, Graber."

7
Bonnie Annie Laurie

For the next three days Parker Quiney did nothing but drive his team north behind the herd. Nate took on his chores for Keeler because of Parker's blistered feet. "I wish ya didn' have ter do all them things," Parker said once to him from the seat, as Nate dumped still another bucket of cow-chips fuel into the wagon back.

"I don't mind," Nate said. "Perhaps someday you'll help me out by taking over my work."

"It appears to me, now that I've pondered on it fer a spell, we been helpin' each other all along," Parker told him. At the sight of Nate's grin, he asked, "Are ya still scared a bringin' Jesse back?"

The grin disappeared at once. "Uh-huh," said Graber. "I'm afraid of dead people, aren't you?"

For a long moment Parker stared out over the prairie as if he were focusing on the grazing, slow-moving *remuda* ahead. But he didn't see the horses at all. He felt again as if a load of snow had dropped down into his gizzard, the way he always felt when he thought about the return journey. "Yep, I'm kinda scared, too." He asked, "You ever seen a ghost, Nate?"

"No, Parker!"

Parker sighed. "Well, we gotta do it all the same. But I reckon we don' have to sleep under the wagon nights comin' back."

On the fourth day after the stampede the herd reached Crawford. There Parker and Nate said good-bye to the cowboys, trail boss, and cook. They weren't given any money for their work, but then, as Nate pointed out, they hadn't used up any of their own supplies at all. Everybody shook hands all the way around.

"*Adios,* leppies," said Keeler, giving Nate some of his precious starter for sourdough bread.

"So long, ya cow buster," Billy Lee told Parker, who got red with pleasure at the praise.

"Thank you very much for everything," said Nate. Parker added, "I'm obliged to ya."

Then, following five of the cowboys bound to town

to celebrate, the boys came into Crawford, a place that was half sod houses and half tents.

"How far is it to Ruination?" Nate asked a whiskery old man slogging down the dusty ruts of the one street.

He said, "Eight, nine days' ride. Jes' follow the Brazos, cross it somewhere's, and head north."

"Did you know any cowboys named Jesse Quiney or Starr Peterson who lived up around there? Did they ever come here to Crawford last year?" Nate wanted to know.

The old man shook his head. "I only been here two weeks. I was run off my place by them Comanche renegades."

Parker and Nate looked at each other wide-eyed. "There's Indians hereabouts?" asked Parker.

"You darn right there is. I seen 'sign' on my land— two gew gaws off their moccasins. Folks say it's Breaks Lances and his brothers. I hear tell they call themselves 'Them That Turns Back.' They jumped the reservation a while back."

"Where is your place?" asked Nate.

"West a here."

"Well, we're northbound."

The old man shrugged. "There's no tellin' where them devil Comanches is by now. Look out fer yerselves, colts." He glanced at the Winchesters under the seat, nodded approval, and went on his way.

Nate looked after him. "He certainly didn't make me feel any better talking about Indians that way."

146

"Nope," Parker Quiney agreed, sounding glum, too. Still, he said, "Giddap" to Pilgrim and Hooraw, who plodded on past the last tent and out onto the green prairie again.

"What do you know about Comanches?" asked Nate, as the coffin slid and rattled against the side of the wagon when the wheel struck a stone.

"Only what Earl told me." Parker tried to make a joke. "You and me, we got plenty to worry about, but old J.E.B. Stuart don'—not one bit. Comanches think a dog's a cousin of a coyote. They won' never kill a dog or Coyote'll get even with 'em and make their young 'uns git sick and die."

"Is that all he told you?"

"Nope, he says Comanches is plenty scared a ghosts, too. They think they turn up when the moon's rising."

Nate Graber gave the sliding coffin a shivering glance, Parker noticed, as the wagon jolted over another rock.

The country along the Brazos was different from the prairie the boys had traveled for so long. There were plenty of trees here, chinaberry, willow, redbud, ash, and elm, as well as wild grapevines and plum bushes. Firewood was plentiful, and the grass was high and sweet for the team. At night the boys camped near the low sandy banks of the red river with the Winchesters always within arms' reach. Parker taught Nate to load and fire his rifle properly—though it was plain as a fly on his nose Graber didn't much take to shooting. When Parker was satisfied Nate wasn't going to blow off his own foot or shoot one of the horses, he said, "If we git attacked by Comanches, the bes' thing fer you ter do is aim for his pony. It's the biggest thing fer a target."

"I couldn't shoot a horse, Parker!" Nate seemed disgusted at the idea. "I don't really think I could shoot anything. I'm like Mr. Peterson. I don't really like guns."

Parker didn't scoff as he might have before he'd heard about Jesse's death and talked to Mr. Peterson. He'd been doin' some ponderin' about guns, too. He said, "A Comanche ain't gonna know that, Nate. You let me do all the aimin' then, while ya make lotsa noise to scare 'em off."

Each twilight when they camped, Parker Quiney prowled around for "sign." On the third night he found it—a piece of red-brown hair near the bank of the Brazos next to a hoofprint in the river sand. With the hair he hurried back to Nate, who waited beside the team, his rifle cradled in his arms, trying to look fierce.

Parker shoved the thing into one of Nate's hands. Nate let out a yelp and dropped it at once. "That's a scalp," he screeched.

Parker stooped and picked it up "Yep, I reckon it is." Then he told of the hoofprint and said, "It was a Indian pony. It didn't have no shoe. I reckon it was fresh sign, but I dunno."

"What are we going to do, Parker?"

"One of us'll keep watch all night and try to keep J.E.B. awake ter give us warnin'."

The terrified boys took turns that night sitting awake under the wagon and prodding the dog into an unwilling alertness. At daybreak J.E.B. Stuart collapsed into a snoring, boneless carcass and they put him into the wagon to rest with his head on a sack of beans.

Hungry because they hadn't dared make a fire, they started out on another day's journey. This time they rode silent and scared until Nate, who'd slept an hour longer than Parker, suddenly split the other boy's eardrums with a yell, "Hey, Parker, look over there!"

Parker, who had been drowsily watching Pilgrim's tail whisking around after a pesty fly, jerked full awake. There south of the river, a half mile away he saw a tall windmill.

"There's folks where a windmill is. They'd mos' likely know about them Comanches." Parker turned the team away from the river. A few minutes later he added, "There's a house there."

"Oh, I just hope there's somebody living in it right now." Nate started to smile. "There's somebody home, Parker! There's smoke coming out of the chimney."

The house near the Brazos wasn't like the ranchhouses in Santa Rosa County. Even if it was good size, it was a sod house. Whoever'd built it had dug a hole four foot deep in the prairie, raised sod walls up to a man's waist, and laid a ridgepole over them, then some brush and sod and dirt. This house had buffalo clover growing on its roof. There was a fence made out of white buffalo bones around a sort of yard. Just startin' up, green corn grew inside the fence. Flowers nodded near the corn, tall white ones, while red roses sprawled on the ground. As Parker Quiney stared at them, surprised because they weren't wild flowers, a girl came out from under a hackberry tree, her hands filled with the white lilies.

"Hello," she said, walking toward them.

Both boys gawked at her. A little gal like her out in Comanche country! It couldn't be!

She smiled and took off her blue-check sunbonnet. "I'm Bonnie Annie Laurie Parrington. You're welcome. Who are you boys?"

Parker clawed off his hat at the same moment Nate did. "I'm Parker Quiney, ma'am," he told her, still popeyed with amazement to find a girl there. She was the purtiest pullet he'd ever laid eyes on—handsome as a heifer in a bed of yellow roses, in fact. She had long goldish hair, which for a mercy wasn' frizzled up ugly by curlin' irons, gray-blue eyes, and a smile sweeter'n molasses.

"I'm Jonathan Graber," Parker heard Nate tell her. Nate added, pointing to J.E.B. Stuart, who'd come alive when he heard the girl's voice and stuck his head over the wagon's side, "This is Parker's dog."

"He looks to be a very nice dog," said the girl. Then she turned around and called out, "Father, Mother!

150

We have some more company." She waited, her face half buried in the lilies. "Where were you going?"

"Up to Whiskey Creek on an errand of mercy," said Nate.

Parker thought Nate was getting pretty high-toned. He guessed what he was up to—gettin' all of the pullet's attention. "We're goin' ter git my brother, who got hisself killed, and take him back to Santa Rosa County for proper buryin', ma'am." As a man and a woman started out of the house, Parker leaned down and said, "Comanches are hangin' around here." He guessed that ought to interest her plenty. "A gal like you shouldn't oughta be out here alone," he warned.

Bonnie Annie Laurie giggled. "Oh, you must mean Breaks Lances."

Her answer irked Parker. Whoever heard of such a thing? He decided to teach the girl a lesson for laughing. He took the piece of hair he'd found out of his shirt pocket and showed it to her. "We found this here scalp jes' a little bit north a here."

The girl didn't scream and run the way he'd guessed she would. She sashayed right up to the wagon, reached up, and took it from his hand. Then she giggled after she'd looked at it and returned it. "Oh, that! It's only a piece of a buffalo's beard. Comanches wear them sometimes on the heels of their moccasins."

Parker Quiney was silent with embarrassment and anger at her. Nate rescued him. "It certainly looked like a scalp to us, ma'am."

151

"Well, it isn't, sillies."

By now the man and woman were there. They were a tall couple with fair hair and grayish eyes like their daughter's. "I'm Emmett Parrington," the man said. "This is my wife Jane. What are you lads doing all the way up here?"

Once more Parker explained his mission. A little flustered now he added, "Seein' Comanche sign made us come outa our way to yer place."

Parrington spoke to his wife, not to Parker. "Whatever he saw must have come from Breaks Lances' band, dearest. Remember, he told me a couple days ago that he was going to cross the Brazos?"

"You been talkin' with *Comanches?*" Parker cried in disbelief.

"Oh, yes. We've known Breaks Lances and his family for quite a while. They used to trade us their very excellent pemmican for corn," explained Mrs. Parrington in a gentle voice.

"But he didn't stay long with us this time. We didn't have any books to give him," Bonnie Annie Laurie volunteered.

"*Books?*" It was Nate's turn to sound astonished.

"Oh, yes. Comanches like to stuff their shields with paper to reinforce them and keep out Kiowa arrows. We like our books too much to have that happen to them. Breaks Lances doesn't understand yet about books."

Parker leaned toward Nate and whispered, "These folks are *loco,* Graber. We better git outa here."

Nate paid him no heed. "Have you got a lot of books?" he asked eagerly.

"Indeed we have, young man," Parrington told him. "Before we came here from the East to try to grow some new varieties of grain, we were both school-teachers."

"Holy Snakes," grumbled Parker so low the Parring-tons didn't hear him. "This here's a nest a wisdom bringers."

"I like books. My father and mother were teachers, too," said Nate.

"Do you like books, young man?" Mrs. Parrington asked Parker.

He told her, "The truth a the matter, is, I like horses better." He fumbled with his hat. "We'll be gettin' on our way now."

Parrington asked suddenly, "Stay for supper, please. We see so few people out here."

Parker glanced at Nate, who was still gawking at the pullet with the posies. "Ya want ter, Nate?"

"Uh-huh. I think we ought to be polite." Then he looked pleadingly at Parker. "Maybe we ought to stay a couple of days and give those Comanches plenty of time to get where they were going."

Already Graber was getting down out of the wagon to smell the lilies and start buttering up the girl.

153

"Where'll I put my horses?" Parker asked the Parringtons.

"Back in the shed. One of our hired men is there. He'll look after them."

As Nate walked toward the house with the pullet and her parents, J.E.B. Stuart left the wagon in one flying leap. Parker looked after him sourly, and muttered, "Go on, dog. Chase after them wisdom bringers, too."

"There'll be chicken for supper," Parker heard Mrs. Parrington call out to him as he took Pilgrim and Hooraw past the sod house.

The boy muttered some more. There'd been chicken at old hell-roarer Symonds place, too. Well, it was all right with him if Nate wanted to hole up here a couple of days to let the Comanches put some prairie between them, but Parker Quiney wasn't going to sleep anyplace where there was a lock on the door. For that matter he wasn't at all sure it wouldn' have been wiser to be known as Ulysses and Sam Houston here, too!

There was no lock on the door of the little room the Parringtons assigned him and Nate, and the chicken was even better than the lady blacksmith's. There were only a couple of things wrong as far as Parker Quiney could see. Mrs. Parrington wouldn't let J.E.B. Stuart sleep on the bed with him and Nate, and the house was full of books, which Nate stuck his nose into with the pullet next to him right after he'd lined his flue with dumplings the first night.

154

From the bed the second night Parker complained, "You and them danged books and that gal! Ya know I ain't got no more use for books than a hog does fer a sidesaddle."

Nate mumbled sleepily, "Maybe when you learn to read, you won't feel that way."

"Nothin' short of a good buffaloin' on the head with a gun barrel'd make me do that, Graber."

Parker minded his manners with the Parringtons, who still seemed sort of *loco* to him, but he felt at home with the hired men, T. J. and Luke. Both were former Confed'rate soldiers. He spent as much time as possible jawin' with them—even if they were sodbuster grain growers, not cowboys. They were often in the shed as there wasn't a lot for them to do in late spring.

"What'd Parrington do in the war?" he asked once.

"He said he was up in Canada learnin' about wheat and things like that," explained sandy-haired T. J.

"Then he come out here and started farmin'," added bush-bearded Luke.

"What's he doin' all the way out here by hisself? Don' he want no neighbors? Did he whip a tired horse up here?" demanded the boy.

Luke knew what he meant—was Parrington a "wanted man." He laughed so hard Parker blushed. "He ain't hidin' out, but he don' seem to hanker after neighbors. It's hard on the little gal, though, and the missus. There ain't no play pretties for Bonnie Annie Laurie, and there ain't no pie suppers for her maw.

But her maw teaches her so she can go away ter high school, they calls it, and then mebbe on ter college."

"Holy Gatlins!" The straw Parker had been chewing on dropped to the barn floor. A gal doin' that! No man he'd ever knowed had gone to school so much. Not even Nerissa with all her fancy airs!

"Purty gal, ain't she?" asked T. J., grinning.

"Mighty so," Parker told him truthfully. Bonnie Annie Laurie seemed to watch him pretty good when he rode her pa's horses aroun' showin' off—though there wasn' a one a 'em he'd call "forked lightning." He hoped Graber wouldn' put a flea in her ear about his not being able to read. "Can ya read?" he asked the farmhands now.

"Sure, Parrington taught us last year," said T. J., hauling a book out of a barrel. "This here's some Shakespeare plays. They're hard goin', but I ain't givin' up. Luke's readin' the Bible."

"Cover to cover, 'Genesis' to 'Revelations,' " said old Luke.

Bonnie Annie Laurie sashayed up to a bored Parker a couple mornings later as he leaned on the buffalo-bone fence staring at the Parrington corn. She was singing to herself in a high, pretty voice. "Hello, Parker," she said.

"Uh-huh," was the best he could think of. Then he asked, "Don' you folks never do nothin' but read books?"

She giggled. "Well, there isn't much else to do. That's how I get away from here—in books."

Parker scoffed. "There ain't no way to ride away on a book!"

"Oh yes, there is! Books are better than horses. They can take you to wonderful places—galloping too. I've been to fairyland and places in Arabia and King Arthur's court."

Parker wanted to spit, but he didn't. That was something Nerissa didn't take kindly to. He was pretty sure this gal wouldn't neither. So he swallowed and said not a word.

"Parker, I want to show you something."

"What?"

"A sapling Father planted to see if it would grow out here. It's a birch from back East."

The back-East tree was behind the house and, to Parker's way of thinking, nothing that could hold a candle to a Santa Rosa County pecan. "Looks to me like it's doin' poorly—mighty skinny, ain't it?"

"Father says it's doing very well," she disagreed. "Birch trees are always slender."

Bonnie Annie Laurie touched the silver bark. "Parker," she said, sounding like the Baptist Church choir down home when it hit the right sound.

The heifer calf's smile made Parker's heart flop over. When it settled back, he said, "Yep."

"Have you got a pocket knife, Parker?"

"Sure, I play mumble peg with it."

157

Bonnie Annie Laurie's gray-blue eyes were melting. "Can you carve things with it?"

"Course I can. You want me to whittle some on yer pa's tree?"

"Just a little bit. It won't hurt it. Can you carve your initials for me?"

"Anybody can do that." Parker took out his knife, opened it, and carved "P" and "Q." "That what you want?" he asked.

She told him softly, "Put a heart around them, a great big one, please."

Parker blushed, but he did what she wanted, digging out a lopsided heart. But as he finished the last bit with his blade, a very awful thought hit him. He backed off from the tree, not looking at the girl. "I gotta go see ta my team now," he muttered.

"But you aren't finished yet, Parker!" said Bonnie Annie Laurie. "Aren't you going to put in my initials, too?"

"Naw, that ain't for me to do." Parker handed her his knife. "You put 'em in if ya want to."

The girl looked mighty surprised. "Mother says men always do all the carving! You put in the 'B' and 'A' and 'L' and 'P.' "

Desperate, Parker said, "Not down in Santa Rosa County they don'. Gals carve out their own!"

"But I want you to do it, Parker!"

"No, ma'am. I tended to my 'Ps' and 'Qs'—that's all I'm gonna do. Yer bein' a forward female."

158

Bonnie Annie Laurie jammed Parker's knife back into his hand, put her apron up to her face, and ran back toward the house, sobbing.

Feeling lower than a rattler's belt buckle, Parker closed his knife and started for the shed. The only good thing outa that was that the pullet hadn' found out he didn' know any more a the alphabet than his own initials. Dammit! He'd took to that pullet too.

A week went by and then another with neither Parker nor the girl mentioning the tree and the incomplete carving. Parker spoke straight out though to Nate a couple of times about leaving, but each time he did the other boy didn't want to go yet. First, he said he wanted to give the Comanches all the time they needed to get out of the country, and then said he'd had a bad dream about the job ahead on Whiskey Creek. But the last time he confessed that he was halfway through *Uncle Tom's Cabin* again, and he didn't want to go until he finished it.

This reason stung Parker to the quick. "That there's a damyankee book. I heard tell about it plenty down home. Anybody who's got that book ain't no real friend to any Quiney," he exploded, "but I don' think that's the real reason why we're still settin' on our backsides here. Yer hangin' aroun' 'cause of the purty pullet."

"Well, aren't you?" Nate slammed shut the book he'd been reading.

"Naw," Parker lied. "I don' stand no show on her

159

string. She's a wisdom bringer, too. I guess ya went and told her I can't read, huh?" It seemed to him the girl was actin' pretty cool to him these days.

"No, I didn't." Nate was angry now, too. "I was ashamed to."

"You was ashamed—ashamed a somebody who rode a steer in a stampede. When I told her what I done, she said I was wonderful." Parker turned on his heel and stomped away to the barn, entirely forgetting to take his hat off to Mrs. Parrington as he went by.

After supper that night things finally came to a head. Mr. Parrington said, "Boys, my wife and I don't see any reason why you two have to go up to Whiskey Creek. I can send T. J. and Luke with your coffin. They wouldn't mind."

Parker was silent while everyone waited. Then he shook his head. "Naw, I gotta do it. My brother Earl's sendin' me. Earl would—"

To Parker's surprise Nate burst in on his speech. "Why not, Parker? Why not?"

"Yes, why not?" came sweetly from Bonnie Annie Laurie. "Then both of you boys could stay here with us while they're gone. We have so many books you've never seen—new books from the East."

Parker said not a word, but only glanced from face to face. The *loco* Parringtons were looking hopefully at him. Bold as brass, so was that scrub, Graber, who ought to have understood how it was with Quineys. "I'll think on it," promised Parker.

160

Bonnie Annie Laurie

"Well, while you think, I'll read out loud to us all."
Mr. Parrington got up, lit the kerosene lamp, and settled himself near a table with a book. Mrs. Parrington
slipped a china egg into a sock and started darning,
while Nate and Bonnie Annie Laurie sat together on
a small sofa. Trapped, Parker crouched in a rocking
chair, glaring down at his boots.

"This is Homer's *Odyssey*," announced the man. "I
think you'll like the story of Circe, the enchantress
who changed men into swine. The hero Ulysses had to
stay on her island for a year."

As Parrington read, Parker fixed his gaze on fat
Graber, who stuffed his face all the time with bear-sign
doughnuts and kept rolling his eyes at the pullet next
to him. Finally disgust made Parker get up and clomp
out, even if the man was readin' on about this Greek
with a damyankee name.

Outside Parker paused, fuming, then stared up at the
moon. It was three quarters again. That meant he'd
been gone from Cottonwood two whole months now.
He leaned against the side of the house, thinking about
what the man had been reading. It made Parker snort!
Heifers and hogs! That was what it was all about. That
scrub Graber'd been roped and tied proper. He'd hang
aroun' a whole year, too, onto that yellow-headed pullet's apronstrings.

Parker went to the shed to see how the team and
J.E.B. Stuart were. He hadn't expected to find Luke
there, but the man was, mending some harnesses.

Parker sat down on a bale of hay. "What d'ya know about Comanches?" he asked.

For an hour the hired man talked to him about Indians. Then Parker said, "Much obliged," and got up into his wagon.

"You gonna sleep in there?" asked Luke, as he hung the harness he'd repaired on the wall.

"Mebbe I am." Parker looked around the wagon. There was the buryin' box, the sacks of supplies, and the Winchesters. J.E.B. Stuart was asleep on some old gunnysacks on the shed floor. The team's harness was hanging from nails on the wall, and Hooraw and Pilgrim were in stalls. All that he needed was right there.

Parker waited until Luke had gone to the little sod shanty he shared with T. J., then came down. He hitched the team, put J.E.B. into the wagon, and cautioned him not to bark. Finally he opened the shed door, hoping it wouldn't creak.

It made only a little bit of noise in the night, but that was enough. As Parker took the wagon out into the moonlight, he saw two black figures coming toward him. He stiffened. No, they weren't tall enough to be the Parringtons or the hired men.

"We heard the shed door," came Nate's voice, then the gasp. "You were going without *me,* Parker?"

"It appears that way, don't it, you scrub?"

"That isn't right of you, Parker, to go on like this," scolded the girl.

"You hush up, you Circe. This here's between me an' him."

"Parker, why don't you let the hired men go up to Whiskey Creek for us?" asked Nate.

"Because Earl sent *me* to do it—not no dead-rank strangers!"

"Maybe there'll be Indians up there," warned Nate.

"Mebbe so, but if you ain't got the grit ter go along —well, I don' want ya."

"You're a pig-headed fool," exploded Graber.

This insult was too much for Parker. Dropping the reins and leaping to the ground, he ran at Nate and hit him in the stomach, then on the mouth. "Pig, huh?" he said, as he went on punching. "The only one around here's you, ya damyankee. She's been sloppin' one hog I know plenty good. Yer more yellow than mustard!"

Nate was fighting, too. One of the blows caught Parker on the nose, another on one eye. Bonnie Annie Laurie let out a little bleat and hotfooted it to the house, to tell her pa, Parker suspected. He picked Graber up by the shirt, hit him twice more, and dropped him. In the moonlight the blood on Parker's fist looked black instead of red. He didn't know if it was his or Nate's and he didn't care either, but somebody was bleedin' like a stuck steer. Parker decided it was time for him to hightail it outa there before that hogmaker female came back with her pa.

As Parker started up onto the wagon seat, he realized Nate was getting up on the other side. He mumbled angrily, "Ain't ya had yer wishbone scratched up enough yet, you varmint? Git away. Ya got snake's blood. I don' want ya. What ya think yer doin'?"

"I'm going to Ruination with you!"

Parker put out a foot and tried to push Nate off, but the other boy grabbed it by the high heel, held on, and twisted the foot.

"Let go a me! Yer *loco*!" Parker yelled.

"I won't let go. I said I was going with you and I am!"

Parker tried to shake free before Nate busted his ankle, but he couldn't manage. Then he heard the door of the sod house open and saw the girl come out, running. Nobody was after her. Nate saw her, too. All at once he let go of Parker's foot, and both crawled up onto the wagon seat.

Bonnie Annie Laurie had two white bundles with her, two things wrapped in table napkins they looked like to Parker.

"Didn' ya bring yer pa?" Parker asked her.

"He's gone to bed. So has Mother." The girl stood on tiptoe and gave one bundle to Nate. "I'm so glad you stopped fighting. That was very disgraceful. This is for breakfast for both of you. Bend down, Jonathan." When he did, Parker heard a smacking sound. She'd kissed the scrub on the cheek! Parker grabbed the reins ready to start the team out and boot Graber off when he wasn't expectin' it, but before he could Bonnie

164

Annie Laurie had run around the horses to his side of the wagon.

"Parker," he heard her say, "this is a berry pie. It's for you. Now you bend over, too."

"Nope," Parker told her, but he took the pie and put it on the seat between him and Nate all the same. Bonnie Annie Laurie was too quick for him, though. She put one foot on a wheel spoke, stepped up on it, wound both of her arms around Parker's neck, and gave him a kiss that tasted of cooky crumbs.

"Good-bye, Parker. God bless you. If you see Breaks Lances, tell him hello from me. Tell him you're friends of mine, and don't let him hurt you. I'll tell Father you felt you had to go. He'll understand. I do." In another instant she was on the ground again, waving good-bye.

"Holy Gatlins. Holy Gatlins, ya sure can't never tell about calico!" Then Parker said to Nate, "Ya can git out here, Graber, and go on back."

"No. I'm going with you! There'll be lots of time for me to be with the Parringtons later on."

"How come ya say that?"

"After you left mad tonight, they asked me to come live with them. They know about my father probably being dead and the Widow Bybee. They're going to give me a letter to the judge in Cottonwood when we come back through here from Whiskey Creek."

"They want ya to move in with 'em?" Parker couldn't believe it.

"Yes, they do."

"How come they didn' ask me, too?"

"They know how many of you Quineys there are. You aren't the same kind of orphan I am. You're the lucky kind."

Parker spat over the wagon side. "There ain't no lucky leppies." He was chewin' some bad cud. Graber was going to live with the Parringtons. Well, that settled his hash. He'd been thinkin' of coming back north when he was a rough-string rider and seein' that pullet agin if she hadn't took off fer college. With Graber livin' there with her, nobody else'd ever make any show on her string. "What's it gonna take fer me ter git shed a ya, Graber?" asked Parker.

Nate didn't reply. Parker stared at him and saw that he held a bandanna to his mouth. He reckoned Nate might be about to spit a tooth. Parker went on, enjoying himself more. "Luke told me tonight the only white man that Comanche, Breaks Lances, likes is Mr. Parrington. He thinks Parrington's *loco*, too. Indians don' mind *loco* white folks. Luke says Breaks Lances don' like him at all and told him once that the only good white man's a dead one, and he'd like to lift Luke's hair. Put that deep down in yer gizzard an' ponder it. We ain't at the Brazos yet. There's still time fer ya to git down and run back home ter the pullet."

Parker waited expectantly, but Graber didn't move a muscle. Parker let out his breath, disgusted. It looked to him like they was right back where they'd been before—getting along like bobcats in a gunnysack.

166

8
Tonkawa

When daylight came the boys ate on the wagon seat without talking, avoiding looking at each other after the first glance. Each had a black eye. Parker had a sore nose and Nate a split lip. To boot, Parker's hand had been sliced across by Nate's teeth, but it cheered him to see that one of Nate's fangs was wobbling as he bit into the pie.

"How are we going to cross?" Nate asked.

"There's only the two a us, so we can't use ropes and haul the wagon across like a trail boss'd do. You grab the supplies, put 'em up here on the seat, and keep 'em

167

dry with the rifles." Parker reached out and grabbed the napkin the pie had been in. With it and the other one in his hand, he got down. Swiftly he blindfolded the team with the napkins, then got back up.

"Hang on, scrub, and do some prayin' we don' hit no suck holes in the river." Parker drove the horses down to the banks of the red-brown water, singing. When Pilgrim felt the water, he reared and nickered. "Easy. Easy," Parker called out to him.

Very slowly the team waded out into the Brazos, up to their fetlocks, then to their bellies. All at once by the wagon's motion, Parker knew they were swimming. J.E.B. Stuart paddled beside them barking.

"Keep a goin'," whispered Parker Quiney, but at that moment the horses stopped. "Giddap," he cried, but nothing happened. Pilgrim was sinking!

Out of the corner of his eye Parker saw Nate slip over the side of the wagon down into the Brazos. He watched him move along, holding onto the harness until he got to Pilgrim's nosepiece. Graber hauled on it, jerking the horse's head and talking into his ear. Then Pilgrim's head rose up all the way out of the river, and the wagon began to move again with Nate swimming beside the team.

"Holy Gatlins, that scrub's for sure a man to ride a river with," Parker told himself admiringly, as the team came sloshing up onto the north bank. While Nate walked back, dripping, to the wagon, Parker

168

looked behind and around him. The buryin' box was wet, but everything else was jim-dandy dry.

"We done it," he told Nate, who got up onto the seat again as they started forward.

"Uh-huh," was Nate's only comment.

Parker clucked to the team. It appeared to him Nate wasn' ready to talk yet, so danged if he'd say anythin' about the good work he done crossin' over.

The country north of the Brazos was bad, in Parker's estimation. It was full of gullies, the kind you couldn't spot until a team near fell down inside. Avoiding them made him go miles out of the way that day. Near suppertime Parker marked out some trees that would give a little shade. Another gully lay beyond them, a real deep one this time. "We're gonna camp here," he said.

"Are we going to have a fire?" asked Nate.

"Sure. Ya can fry this here rabbit. J.E.B's the only one who can handle it raw." Parker reached under the seat and held up the rabbit he'd shot at midday.

There was enough dry wood under the trees for a fire. It wasn't long before Nate had skinned and cut up the rabbit. Parker tied the team to the wagon after they'd grazed for a while, then came to sit by the fire.

It was a warm June night. The evening star was already out, and some owls were hooting in the distance. Parker lay back, his hands folded behind his head, resting, counting the hoots. Suddenly it seemed to him there was a helluva lot of owls out on one night. He sat up and told Nate quietly, "Don' make no noise, Graber, but I reckon there's Indians aroun' here."

Nate dropped the frying pan he was putting the rabbit into and looked around him. "I don't see anything."

"You wouldn'—if they was Comanches. But I don' think that was owls I was hearin' unless there's a mass meetin' of 'em here."

"Let's go back to the Parringtons."

"We can't," Parker told him through teeth held shut to keep them from chattering and letting Graber know how scared he was. "Them Indians is between us and the Brazos. I reckon they been followin' us for a while."

"Isn't there anything we can do?"

Parker had been thinking about this, too. "Well, we can sure let 'em know we got the Winchesters—two of 'em. They mighta even heard me shoot that rabbit. You and me are gonna fire off the Winchesters a couple times like we was huntin'. We'll walk out a ways from the wagon, then come on back." He saw Nate's trembling lips. "Think ya can do it?"

Nate rose slowly. "I'll try, Parker."

Together, the boys took the rifles out of the wagon. His knees wobbly, Parker walked out into the twilight, his rifle ready. His mouth was too dry to whistle, but he managed to sing in a quavering voice, "My fire I kindle with chips gathered round. My coffee I boil without bein' ground."

170

Tonkawa

From a distance came Nate's voice singing, "Glory Glory Hallelujah. His truth is marching on."

Parker sighted on an imaginary target along the gully's rim and fired. A moment later he heard the second rifle blasting away, sending a yellow bird into the sky crying "kill-dee, kill-dee."

Parker fired again, and so did Nate. Then Parker went back with J.E.B. Stuart at his heels. He looked down at the dog and sighed. At the fire he told Nate, who'd beat him back, "I jes' wish I could get old J.E.B. to do some howlin'. Luke told me that a wolf howlin' would make Comanches stop whatever they was fixin' ter do."

Nate eyed the dog doubtfully. "He'll keep quiet when you tell him to."

"Uh-huh," agreed Parker, "but nobody ever taught him to howl."

"Maybe he'll do it naturally when the moon comes up."

"Naw, Earl and me broke him a doin' that so's we could sleep."

Parker sank onto his haunches. "Start up that rabbit, Nate. We gotta look as natcheral as we can, and we gotta eat ter keep our strength up. I don't reckon we're gonna do any more sleepin' at the same time 'till we git to Ruination. That coffee made yet?"

Parker reached into the coals to the coffeepot just as Nate said, "Here, let me do that." Nate already

171

had his hand outstretched for the pot, as Parker picked it up. Suddenly it tipped in Parker's grasp, the lid fell off, and coffee flooded over Nate's hand in a boiling torrent.

Nate grabbed at his scalded hand with the other one and doubled over on the ground with pain. He didn't let out one yelp, though.

Parker put down the pot and caught up the water bucket. He hauled Nate up, grabbed at the injured hand, and shoved it down into the cool water. Firelight shone on the huge tears rolling down Nate's face.

"Is that better?" asked Parker.

"No, it's terrible," moaned Nate.

"Keep yer hand in there, ya hear me." Parker left Nate with J.E.B. Stuart whining next to him. There was a tin bucket of axle grease in the wagon. He'd spread that on the burn. But before he found the bucket, he ran across something else in a sack, the four bottles of Professor Tyree's elixir. Parker brought one of them to the fire instead of the grease. Tyree had said it was good for whatever ailed the human carcass. And Earl always swore by whiskey as a pain-killer. Parker knew the Seminole Elixir was full of it.

Parker uncorked it, holding his breath, then handed it to Nate. "Here, take a couple swallows a this. Then ya won' hurt so bad."

He watched Graber tilt the bottle and drink, then heard him coughing. The elixir was a third gone when

172

he gave the bottle back to Parker. "The whiskey'll help," Parker told himself out loud, but he had to admit he wasn't so sure about the gunpowder.

Sitting by the fire with the Winchesters, watching Nate, Parker cussed his luck. If it wasn' Comanches, it was somethin' else. He didn't know which was the worst thing on his mind right now—the Indians or Graber. After a time he saw Nate take his hand out of the bucket and fall back onto the ground. The sky was completely dark now. In a little while the moon would be out. Parker watched Graber carefully. "How's yer hand?" he asked.

Nate didn't answer; he only hiccupped.

"Think ya can fry the rabbit now, Nate?"

Graber shook his head, giggling. His face was gettin' sort of red, Parker noticed.

"Ya want ter play mumble peg, Nate? J.E.B. can have the rabbit. We still got some a the pie the pullet give us."

"I don't want anything," mumbled Nate, getting up. "Holy Gatlins, you Rebel, why don't you ever leave anybody alone? You've been pestering me ever since we left Cottonwood. I can't do anything to suit you. I'm sorry for your sister-in-law, Nerissa. She's the rough-string rider in your family, not you. All of you Quineys are half-broken mules! I don't know why I ever took up with an ignorant scrub like you. You're *proud* of being ignorant." After this speech, which left

Parker drop-jawed it was so unexpected, Nate lurched over to the wagon. He climbed inside it, went down behind the sides, and didn't come out again.

Parker sat alone by the fire, astonished by the outburst. Then he called out, "Nate, Nate." When there wasn't any answer, he went to the wagon, carrying his rifle. There, next to the coffin, curled up on his side, lay Nate snoring. "Lord A'mighty," breathed Parker Quiney. "That's sure some elixir."

Shaking his head, Parker hauled out what was left of the pie at Nate's head and got under the wagon with it and the rifle. Then he remembered the second Winchester by the fire, crawled out, and fetched it and the rabbit back, too. Nate wasn't any use to him now. J.E.B. might as well have the rabbit.

While J.E.B. crunched bones, Parker thought about what Nate had said about Nerissa. He guessed that was how she thought of herself, all right. "You git on jes' fine with her, don' ya?" he asked J.E.B. once, feeling lonesome. But the dog didn't even look at him. It was near moonrise now. Tuckered out again, J.E.B. had put his head between his paws and gone to sleep. There'd sure be no howlin' tonight.

Parker leaned against a wagon wheel, listening. There weren't any more owl hoots, only Nate's snores, J.E.B.'s soft breathing, and the nibbling sounds the horses made as they grazed on the grass within their reach. The boy pondered Earl's and Luke's words about Comanches. Bein' so scared at first had put

them right out of his mind. No, the Indians wouldn'
come at him and Nate at night. If they'd been going to
rush 'em, they woulda done it before dark. They be-
lieved if one of 'em got killed at night, his spirit wouldn'
be able to find its way to heaven. Besides Comanches
were leery of ghosts, which showed up with the risin'
moon.

But on the other hand, nobody could ever be sure
about Indians! Breaks Lances had been around white
folks a lot. Mebbe he'd took on some white men's ways
a thinking. Parker reckoned he'd have to stay awake
all night. He gave a mean look at the wagon bottom
and then at his dog. There sure wasn't no help comin'
from either of them two.

While Parker Quiney kept watch, the moon rose
and started its climb into the sky. Everything was silver
and black now except for the fire that was dying down
and smoking grayer than the grass. A little later J.E.B.
Stuart woke up, scratched a flea, crawled over and put
his head onto Parker's knees, and went to sleep again.
For a time Parker hummed to himself to keep awake,
but finally his head slumped forward onto his chest.

The dog's twitching during a rabbit-chasing dream
awakened the boy. Annoyed, he started to push J.E.B.
off him the way he always did when the dog took up
too much of the bed. Then he remembered with a start
where he was and looked out from under the wagon.
He caught his breath, terrified.

There was a man on horseback a hundred feet away.

As Parker watched, he slid off his pinto and started forward over the grass. Parker rolled over onto his belly and put the Winchester to his cheek.

The man was an Indian. His hair was in long braids with a feather at the back. His earrings made out of seashells shone in the moonlight. Parker saw other glintings on the Indian's leggings, bits of silver and more shells. His buckskin shirt had beads of white and some dark color Parker couldn't identify all over its front.

"It's Breaks Lances hisself," Parker whispered to himself. He nodded. He knew what the Comanche was after—Hooraw and Pilgrim. The Indians must have thought he and Nate were asleep. Stealing tied-up horses in a enemy camp showed off a Comanche's grit almost as much as takin' a scalp in battle. They wouldn' fight at night, but they'd git horses if they could. That's how Comanches showed how rich they were—by the number of horses they owned. Luke'd said they called horses "god dogs."

Parker aimed the rifle, his finger ready on the trigger. Old Breaks Lances wasn' going to get no Quiney horse. Parker would wait till the Indian cut one of 'em loose, then he'd shoot him.

Closer and closer the Indian came. Parker could see the streaks of light-colored paint on his face. As he approached the wagon, Parker saw him take a long, gleaming knife from his belt. Still Parker waited. The time to pull the trigger was when the Indian was right

176

next to the horse he was gonna take first. Pilgrim and
Hooraw must be asleep on their feet or they woulda
snickered because of their nearness to the Indian pony.

Parker was astonished how silent the Comanche
was. He was right next to the wagon where Parker
could count the silver pieces on his leggings. Now was
the time to crawl out and shoot!

Then all of a sudden he heard Nate turn over.

"Ai-ee-ee-ee!" came the Comanche's yowl an instant
later. Shrieking, the Indian started running toward his
pony.

Parker squeezed off a wild shot, but missed. Still
yelling, the man jumped onto his horse, swung the
pinto around, and disappeared from sight, sliding over
the gully's rim. Parker got out from under the wagon
and looked inside it, hoping the Comanche hadn't
knifed Nate. There was Graber, lying on his back, his
hands folded peacefully over his chest, jes' the way
folks got laid out for burying back in Santa Rosa
County. Out of respect Parker took off his hat, then
he looked Nate over for wounds, but there didn't seem
to be any.

"Graber!" he called out.

Nate didn't open his eyes and started to snore again.

Laughing, Parker Quiney got out Nate's quilts and
covered him up. It was his horseback opinion that
Graber wouldn't be worth a plugged nickel to him
tomorrow. The elixir'd see to that. Parker'd have all
the work to do, so he'd better get what shut-eye he

could. He needn't worry about Comanches anymore, he reckoned. Parker got down his own bedroll, hauled an excited dog into it with him, and went to sleep, smiling.

Parker was wrong about Nate. He was up at dawn, bushy-tailed and bright-eyed, shaking Parker awake.

"There's been a horse around here," he shouted into Parker's ear.

"I know. I reckon it was Breaks Lances."

Nate was startled. "But you slept, Parker—with Comanches roaming around us!" Nate's eyes were fierce and accusing.

"There ain't no Comanches here now. How's yer hand?"

"A little swollen and sort of red, but it's all right."

Parker, whose head buzzed from lack of sleep asked sourly, "Ain't you hurtin' nowheres—mebbe in yer head? You oughta. You drank plenty a Tyree's elixir."

"No." Nate shook his head violently from side to side, something Earl always avoided doing when he'd "cut his wolf loose" in a saloon.

"It jes' has ter be the gunpowder," Parker told himself. He slid back down into his bedroll, but not before he said, "Start up the fire. Give me a call when it's time for chow."

"But Parker," Nate protested, "you haven't explained to me about the hoofprints around here, and you said something about Comanches!"

178

Parker spoke from under his quilts. "Far as the Comanches go, they sure don' want ter set eyes on you! One a 'em spotted ya last night in back a the wagon with our buryin' box when he come to steal my horses. You scared him plenty!"

"Me? Scared a *Comanche Indian?"*

"Yep." Parker stuck his head out for the last time, he hoped. "The Indian reckoned you was dead, but when ya moved, he thought you was a ghost that come with the moon risin'. Nate, quit yer worryin' about them Comanches. I reckon ya got rid of 'em right and proper. There ain't a Comanche in twenty miles a here by now in any direction."

Nate looked shattered to his shoelaces by this news. Then he asked, shuddering, "How did I get up there next to the coffin, Parker?"

"All by yer lonesome, Graber. Ya climbed up full a Seminole Elixir and nested down next ter it real neighborlike. I covered ya up after the Comanche skedaddled. Now go fix the fire and forgit about that rabbit. J.E.B. ate that up las' night. Far as I see, we got a easy road ahead ter Ruination now. Lemme git some shut-eye in peace, will ya?"

Another three days of traveling in the hot sun took Parker Quiney's good spirits away. It was sure mean country for a man and plenty hard on horses, too, pulling up and down outa one red gully after another and sometimes going around the deepest ones.

Parker and Nate were both irritable when they stopped at sunset the third night. "Don' ya give me the fat part off the bacon agin," snapped Parker.

"You haven't been getting any more fat than I have!" was Nate's heated reply. "If you don't want to eat bacon anymore, shoot a rabbit or prairie hen. You know I can't hit anything with that buffalo gun of yours."

Parker told him, "Those ain't buffalo guns. They're what a real Texan'd carry."

Nate scoffed, "Go ahead, tell me I'm not a real Texan!"

Parker sighed, but said nothing. He was still pondering what Nate had said two nights before. There was some truth in it. And the truth of the matter, too, was that Graber was a pretty good Texas man. Who'd a thought he'd do the things he did when he'd first took long-curls along? But he'd be danged if he'd give him any credit for scarin' off the Comanche. Any drunk could have done that just as good. "I'll try to git us somethin' else ter eat," said Parker, reaching for the Winchester the minute they'd made camp.

He walked away from Nate. For a while he stood at the edge of another gully, which split the land east and west. Ruination wasn't many miles north, he reckoned. And just beyond there was Whiskey Creek and the chore Earl had set him. Parker tried not to think of the bad dream he'd had about that the night before.

180

A noise caught his attention. It sounded to him like rocks rattling down in the gully. Mebbe it was a rabbit or a coyote. Parker stared down into the shadows below him and saw something moving—something good-sized. It was a horse and a man. Another Indian mebbe? He went swiftly to a boulder and kneeled behind it, holding the rifle ready. Whoever it was was coming up out of the gully. He'd wait for him. The first thing Parker spotted was the top of a black hat, then beneath it a fringe of white hair, and next a wrinkled brown face and washed-out Levi-blue eyes. The rider was a white man and an old one, too.

The boy let the man come up out of the gully. His jacket and boots were old, most nearly as old as his horse, a flea-bitten gray, skinny as a lobo wolf. The stranger's saddle and bridle looked ready to fall to pieces. Even his gun holster was flaky with age. "He's poor as skim milk," Parker told himself contemptuously, and the man had the look of a brand-blotchin' rustler, too.

Parker got up with the Winchester trained on the newcomer. Old rattlers could bite good as young ones. "Who'd you be?" Parker demanded.

Blinking in surprise, the old man raised his hands, "Howdy, boy." His voice was flat and soft. Then he grinned, and Parker saw his bridle teeth were missing.

"I asked ya, what's yer name?"

"It ain't perlite of ya ter ask, but they calls me

181

Tonkawa. I'm the Tonkawa Kid." A breeze across the gully rim made the old man's white hair lift off his collar.

"What's yer last name?"

"William Garland Bailey. Who'd ya be, colt?" The old man grinned again.

"Sam Houston Smith." Parker asked another question. "What're ya doin' out here alone, mister?"

"Goin' down home mebbe. I dunno. Can I put my hands down now, son?"

"Aw right." Parker lowered the rifle and said, "We ain't got no money, so there's no use yer tryin' ter rob me an' my pardner."

The old man seemed hurt by this remark. "There ain't no cause to say things like that ter me, boy."

Ignoring him, Parker asked, "Where'd ya come from?"

"Ruination."

"Did ya know my brother, Jesse?"

"I never heard a him. I was only there yestiday for a little while." The man rose up in his stirrups. "Seems ter me I smelled some coffee?"

Parker said, "Yer welcome ter eat with us, I reckon."

The stranger leaned hopefully out of the saddle. "I'm sure tired a all the alkali water I been drinkin'. Ya wouldn't have no tonsil varnish with ya to cut the taste, would ya?"

The boy shook his head. It was like he figgered— this Bailey was a old whiskey soak, too.

182

The gray horse fell in with Parker as he started toward the wagon. "Are you a buff'lo bone hunter?" he asked.

"Never was!" The old man was angry. "Never will be. Not old Tonkawa."

Parker stared at him, surprised by the show of spunk. The old man's eyes were bright with indignation. "Sure I wore my gun low and used ter think I was the toughest longhorn who ever shook his antlers anywheres. But I wasn' what ya think. I never pecosed a man and never was a dirty buff'lo hunter."

Parker saw how he looked around. The anger was gone now, and he was sad-sounding. "The buff'lo mos' all gone outa these parts now. Injuns is gone, too, I hear tell. I was blood brother to some Tonkawas. I seen 'em herded off ter the reservation back in 1855. A damned shame it was, too—like puttin' 'em in jail. That was when I headed west outa Texas and dropped my name in the river and lost it. I. . . ."

Parker had closed his ears by the time he and the stranger were at the wagon. He saw Nate get up with the skillet of cornbread in his hand. "He says he's named Bailey, Ulysses." Parker added under his breath to Nate, who came around the fire to him, "He calls hisself the Tonkawa Kid."

Nate put the cornbread back into the ashes, reached up, and shook the old man's outstretched hand. "I'm Ulysses Simpson Johnson. I'm pleased to make your acquaintance."

"Likewise," the old man said after he'd dismounted. He was spryer than he looked. Parker caught his sharp glance in his direction. "It's nice ter know there's still some manners left in some Texas young'uns."

"Oh, don't mind Sam Houston. I'm trying to educate him, but he doesn't take to it well yet," said Nate. "I hope you'll be having supper with us, Mr. Bailey."

"Call me Tonkawa," said Bailey. "I been asked by this carrottop here. I'm stayin'." He seemed to study Nate's face as he'd studied Parker's. Nate's black eye had gone from purplish-red to yellowish-green, but it was still there. "Well," he exclaimed, settling himself on the ground, "nobody ever said pardners had ter be good friends, but if they is, it does help some. Down home once my horse tried ta jump over a steer and didn't make it. You'd a thought my pardner woulda picked me up and dusted me off, but not him. I like ta busted ever'. . . ."

Parker hunkered down next to Nate and was silent, but when his dog moseyed over to sniff at the old man, who reached out to fondle his ears, Parker whispered, "He's a old windbelly. I'm gonna sit up and keep a eye on our outfit all night. It appears ter me he'd make off with ever'thing that ain't tied down. Watch out fer that gold piece a yers."

Nate waited while the Tonkawa Kid mumbled on to the dog, then said, "He looks all right to me."

"Not ter me, he don', and fer a stranger he does too much jawin'."

184

Now the old man looked across the fire at Parker. "Where'd ya say ya was goin', redhead?"

"I didn't say, but we're headed fer Whiskey Creek." Parker ordered Nate, "Ya might jes' as well fry up that bacon. It's too close ter dark to git us anythin' else with the Winchester." Parker sat crosslegged, his eyes on the old man, his rifle in his lap.

"What're ya colts gonna do up there?" asked Bailey.

"We're gonna dig up my brother who got hisself killed las' winter and bring him home ter Santa Rosa County fer buryin'."

Parker saw the toothless smile of disbelief. "Ya swing a mighty wide loop, colt."

"If ya don' believe me, go take a look in my wagon. I ain't no flannelmouth." Parker was so angry he said, "My real name's Parker Quiney. His is Nate Graber. Mebbe we're jes' colts, but we ain't folks ta fool with."

There was an angry challenge in the stranger's eyes. He sat silent for a time, then while his horse grazed, he got up and went to look in the wagon. When he came back to the fire, Parker saw the challenge was gone. It had been replaced by a look he couldn't identify. "Uh-huh, I seen yer buryin' box. That's a tall order fer young'uns like you two, ain't it?"

"His brother Earl sent him," explained Nate, who'd poured the old man a cup of coffee and taken it to him around the fire.

"Much obliged," said the Tonkawa Kid, as he stirred the coffee with the barrel of his gun.

Parker relaxed, lowering the Winchester after the man started his peaceful stirring, but all the same didn't take his eyes from him.

The stranger said slowly, "See here, boys. I ain't in no gut-bustin' hurry. I'll go up ta this here Whiskey Creek with ya if ye'll stake me ter grub. Mine's jest about all gone. The way I look at it I oughta do a couple things that're good before I cash in my chips an' go to glory. I oughta try to even things up fer me much as I can." He sighed and sipped, then told the boys, "I done plenty that was bad in my time. If ya'll take me, I'll do fer ya what ya got ter do up there. How 'bout it?"

"No!" came from Parker Quiney.

"Yes!" came at the same instant from Nate Graber.

186

9
The
Line
Camp

As Parker and Nate glared at one another, the Tonkawa Kid put down his cup and said, "You want me
to go away so's ya can make up yer minds in private?"

Parker opened his mouth to say "No" once more,
but Nate beat him to it. "Now you listen to me, you
long-legged donkey. It's plain to me you're no smarter
now than when we started out together. I've tried to
teach you things that mattered, but you haven't learned
one single thing as far as I can see! But I have!" Nate
gestured with the heavy coffeepot and didn't spill a
drop. "I know you've thought all along I was a stupid

187

muley cow without any horns and couldn't butt, but
I scratched your wishbone up plenty, didn't I, back at
Parringtons'? And I've backed you up all the way
along, haven't I? You are an ingrate, Parker Quiney!"

While Nate paused for breath, the old man put in,
"That's what made me turn bad—ingratitude, it was."

Ignoring him, Nate went on, "I've learned how to
do some things from you. I can drive the team nearly
as well as you and hitch nearly as fast, and who was it
who swam the Brazos? Maybe I don't ride like a bronc
snapper, but then how long will you last when you get
to be one? You'll probably kill yourself in ten years.

"You're as conceited as a barber's pug dog. You're
as stubborn as sin. You always have to get your own
way. Pride's the worst thing there is!" Nate paused, his
chest heaving with anger, the stolen hat slipping down
over his ears. He pushed it back and started out this
time in Spanish, *"Burro, estúpido, ignorante. . . ."*

For a time Tonkawa listened, then as Nate's Spanish grew louder and more rapid, the old man started
to laugh. He called out to Parker, furious, across from
him. "He's a ornery cusser, redhead. He ain't called ya
the same thing twice. If ya try answering' him back,
ya'll have more cud than ya can chew!"

Parker got up. "I ain't gonna, old man. I don' know
much Spanish. Ya wanta go on back, ya Yankee
scrub?"

"Not this close, I'm not, Quiney. I'm going to Ruination all right." Nate looked at the old man. "Would

you go back down to Santa Rosa County with me, Mr. Bailey, after we get to Whiskey Creek?"

"I reckon I might, boy."

Nate whirled in triumph. "What do ya have to say to that, Parker?"

"Good riddance. Suit yerself. Let's eat. The cornbread's burnin'."

Supper was quiet. While Parker ate, he kept his eyes on his rifle, thinking. What Graber'd said about pride stuck in his craw. That's what Nerissa was always tellin' him and Leo—how bad a thing pride was. She said she hadn't seen a Quiney yet who wasn' puffed up with it—even the weaner gals. "Independence" was what Earl used to call it, but "plain old sinful pride" was what Nerissa said it really was. Parker stole a glance at the Tonkawa Kid, chasin' a bean around his plate with a piece of bread. He reckoned the old man had done jest about everything there was to do by now, so he could dig up Jesse. Parker sure didn't hanker after doin' it himself, particularly alone. Earl wouldn' find out if Nate didn' tell folks in Cottonwood, and Parker figured he wouldn' if he got his way.

Parker put down his plate, swallowed the last of the bacon fat, wiped his mouth with the back of his hand, and spoke to a brooding Nate. "Aw right, Graber. He can go. I'm givin' in ta ya."

Nate looked up. A smile lit his face. "You mean it, Parker?"

"Uh-huh, but it don' mean I'm glad a yer comp'ny.

189

All it means is that I reckon I owe ya somethin' fer comin' this far with me. Us Quineys pay our debts."

"You certainly do owe me," Nate agreed in a loud voice. He turned to the Tonkawa Kid. "Would you like some more coffee, Mr. Bailey?"

The man held out his cup, grinning. "I don' mind if I do. Ya like fancy shootin', Nate? I used ta be able to ride in ter a town and haul a rifle outa its saddle scabbard, whizz it aroun', cock it with one finger, and shoot out all them round things in a saloon sign."

Nate laughed. "The 'Os' you mean, Mr. Bailey— the letters in 'saloon.' "

"Yep, that's what somebody else told me them was. I can't read, but I used ta could pop a bee off a thistle with a Winchester at sixty paces ridin' fast as my hoss could go. I don' hold with guns much myself no more. Trouble is, ya can never tell what hand a gun's gonna wind up in." He looked mournful for a moment. "But I can't do that kinda shootin' no more. Being where I was the last twenty years took it outa me."

"Where were you?"

"San Quentin jailhouse—out in California ever since '59. I killed a miner out there in the silver fields, an' they got me. I didn't never take ta lettin' daylight through a man. I only been outa there four months. I was born in McMullen County way back in 1819." He tilted his head back to look up into the sky. "I used to have a fiddle when I was a colt yer age. I kep' a snake's rattles in her ta keep out the damp. There

190

wasn' a square dance I didn' go ta, and then one night I spied this here little gal and that there black hoss in. . . ."

Parker sighed. After the McMullen County remark, he'd quit listening again. Earl said that county was plumb popping with outlaws. He reckoned it'd be smart of him to sleep with the Winchesters pretty close to hand again.

Another day of skirting gullies brought the boys and the old man to a town of sod dugouts on a red-dirt street.

Parker called to the Tonkawa Kid riding beside the wagon, "I guess this here's Ruination, huh?"

"Sure is. It ain't much ta look at, but it's got its hair on right enough."

"What does that mean, Mr. Bailey?" asked Nate.

"A damned rough place," Parker translated for him. He flung the reins to the other boy, leaped down, and went inside what he guessed to be a saloon, because there were some empty barrels out front with Xs on them.

This time the bartender didn't try to throw him out. He looked up from sweeping the packed dirt floor. "What d'ya want, kid?"

Parker looked into a corner before answering. There was another man there, sitting at a table, twirling a gun around his index finger, then catching it and aiming. He looked up and gave Parker a tight smile.

191

"How far's Whiskey Creek?" Parker asked the saloonkeeper, but keeping an eye on the gun-twirler.

"Eight miles as the crow flies." The man leaned on his broom. "Ya lookin' fer somebody up there?"

Parker didn't know how to reply. How could you look for somebody dead? "I'm lookin' fer a line camp. My brother, Jesse Quiney, worked there."

"I knowed Jess," said the cowboy with the gun. "He worked fer old Binder. He's the old longhorn who runs the B Triangle spread." There was no "I'm sorry about your brother" from him.

"Where's his ranch, mister?"

"Five miles north."

For an instant Parker was tempted to ask the two men what had happened to make Jesse and Starr Peterson fight, but he didn't like the dugout. It smelled like a dirty barn, and the man who toyed with the hogleg like it was a play pretty made him jumpy. "Much obliged," he told them and got up out of the dugout as fast as he could. Yep, Ruination had its "hair on" all right. Tonkawa could be trusted in some things then.

The country beyond Ruination was open and, for the most part, flat again. Hooraw and Pilgrim made good time, their harness jingling cheerily, but Parker and Nate were silent in the heat of the day. Tonkawa, riding beside them, seemed lost in his own thoughts for a change. The two boys had had words again that night after the Tonkawa Kid had bedded down a distance from the wagon.

Parker'd told Nate, "When it comes to old rattlesnakes you don't know a heifer from a horned frog."

Nate had come back by saying, "Every Quiney who ever came over the pike was as stubborn as a goat and ignorant as a pig and proud as the devil of it."

As they came down off a little hill, Parker saw a rider approaching. He reined in the team and waited for the man, a red-cheeked young cowboy.

"This here's B Triangle property," the cowboy told the Tonkawa Kid.

"We know that," said the old man, "but the redhead's got bus'ness on it."

"I'm Parker Quiney," said Parker. "I come up after my brother, Jesse."

The young cowboy nodded gravely. "We been sort of expectin' ya, Pa and me." He leaned out of the saddle and shook Parker's hand. "I'm Louie O'Hearne. Ya wanta go to Whiskey Creek now? Mr. Peterson's been up there a' ready."

Parker said, "We know. Me and my pardner run across him in Buffalo Notch. Is Whiskey Creek jes' up ahead?"

"Sure is. Ya can't miss the line camp dugout if ya go due north. We only use it wintertimes. There ain't nobody there now. Ya go on up and wait. I'll fetch my pa. He's the foreman wrote ya the letter about Jess.

I knowed him and Starr, too." O'Hearne added in an embarrassed way, "I see ya got a coffin, but do ya need a shovel?"

"Yep," agreed Parker Quiney. He gestured toward the old man. "This here's the Tonkawa Kid."

"Howdy." O'Hearne bobbed his head, then swung his horse about, and called out, "We'll see ya at the line camp."

"Wait a minute," Nate shouted after him, making him rein in. "Mr. Peterson told us there was somebody who talked to Jesse Quiney before he died. Can we see him? He missed seein' him."

"That'd be Amadeo. Yep, he was gone then. I'll fetch him, too."

Parker's heart beat faster every time the wheels turned, and he wanted to jump down and run away and hide. But he didn't waver once travelin' north except to drive out of the way of three little skunks and a big one going due east. He stole a look at Graber. Nate was licking his lips, hanging onto the seat like he was being drove to his own hangin'. Tonkawa didn' seem bothered one bit, though, squinting straight ahead of him.

The line camp was only a little dugout beside a quick-running creek. Parker got down right away.

"Ya want I should come with ya?" asked Tonkawa.

"Naw, wait fer the O'Hearnes." Parker pushed open the door of the dugout and went inside. There wasn't much there—two iron beds, a wood stove, a table with a torn oilcloth on it, chairs, and a skillet. For a long time he stood in the gloom, trying to remember what he could about his brother Jesse, but nothing more would come to him than memories of the ring and the mouth organ.

Parker left the sod house. He found the graves a hundred yards to the west under some mesquite trees. One of them had had the pen of logs around it removed and the rocks taken off. The other one was nice and neat, just the way the cowboys had fixed it. On a tree near them both, somebody had cut the name "Quiney" and what Parker supposed must be "Peterson."

He sat down beside Jesse's grave. After a time Nate came, too, and plopped down next to him saying nothing, only listening to the mournful prairie wind. Finally the boys heard the drum of hooves They got up and went back to the wagon.

Three men rode up. One was young Louie O'Hearne. The fat man who looked like him was his father, Parker guessed, and behind him came a black-haired man with a mustache, who looked Mexican. He had the rope of a little bay mare trailing his horse tied to his saddle horn. All the bay lacked was a rider. The horse had saddle, blanket, bridle, bedroll, and all on her.

"This here's my pa," called out Louie O'Hearne, nodding toward the fat man. "And this is Amadeo Díaz."

Parker shook hands with the newcomers when they dismounted and told them, "Howdy."

Old Mr. O'Hearne seemed mighty uncomfortable while he sized Parker up. Then he gestured toward the riderless horse. "Yer brother's saddle's there and his bedroll. I reckon they're yours. The hoss ain't, though. She belongs to the B Triangle." The man took down the gun belt draped over the saddle horn and held it out. "This was his, too."

"Yes, sir," said Parker, staring at the gun for a long moment. Then he said, "Will ya put Jesse's saddle and stuff in the wagon?"

"Sure, boy." O'Hearne squinted at Parker. "What about his gun and belt?"

"I'll take 'em."

Silently O'Hearne handed Parker the belt and gun, which had plain wood handles. Parker was aware of how everybody stared at him as he put on the belt and buckled it. It felt just as heavy on him as it had in his hand.

O'Hearne let out his breath, and said, "I didn' reckon anybody'd send someone yer age up here."

"I was the biggest one at home."

The man grunted and now started to unlash the shovel and a tarpaulin from where they were tied behind his saddle. When he'd finished, the Tonkawa Kid came up and took them. "I'm doin' that fer the young'uns, mister."

196

"I'm mighty glad to hear it," was the foreman's remark, giving the canvas and shovel to the old man. As Tonkawa walked slowly toward the grave, the two O'Hearnes took down the wagon tail gate, lifted the coffin out, and carried it to the side of Jesse's grave.

"Amadeo, can I talk ta ya?" said Parker.

"*Si, chico.* What do you want to know?"

"I hear tell ya talked to Jess before he died?"

"For a leetle while." Amadeo squatted down near to the trickle of red water that was Whiskey Creek with Parker while Nate sprawled on the grass. "I heard shootin' and come up here to see if they was shootin' at lobo wolves. The lobos they were very bad last winter after the calves. Starr, he was dead when I come here." The Mexican crossed himself. "Your brother was dying, and I talked to heem."

"Did Jesse kill Peterson over a heifer by the name a Lily Bass?" demanded Parker.

"A gorl?" Amadeo shook his head. "No gorl! Eet was a fight over who was the bes' *soldado.*"

"Soldier?" came from Nate.

"*Si,* that is eet. Was eet General Beauregard or was eet General Stuart who was the bes'?"

"They was *both* Confed'rate generals!" exploded Parker.

"That ees how eet was, *muchacho.*"

"Holy Gatlins, That's *loco!*" Parker wailed.

"*Si, es loco.*" Amadeo shook his head.

197

Parker stared at the creek, stupefied. Fighting and killing each other over something like that! Why, the Petersons had been Confed'rates, too!

He heard Nate's quiet voice. "That sort of sounds like you and me, Parker, doesn't it?"

"You're a Yankee—I ain't. We got cause to fuss."

"Oh, Parker. I've been thinking about this ever since we left Cottonwood. There aren't any real Yankees anymore or any more real Johnny Rebs. The war's been over for fourteen years. Won't anybody in Texas ever forget it?" Nate paused. "We weren't even born yet when it had already ended. And Jesse and Starr didn't fight in it either. They were too young."

Parker fought tears, listening to the sounds of Tonkawa's shoveling. Amadeo broke the long silence, "Eet was *estúpido.*"

"*Estúpido,* and they both had guns," was Nate's melancholy addition.

Now the two O'Hearnes came back and joined the boys and the Mexican by the water.

"Was Jess a good hand?" Parker asked the B Triangle foreman.

"I couldn' have asked for no better workers than him and Starr. I'd never thought this'd happen, or I'd never put 'em together all winter out here ta keep the cows from driftin' off the range. They gen'rally went along a hundred fifty percent together." O'Hearne's voice was brighter. "Like you two colts do."

Parker Quiney felt the heat of a blush starting at his

collar, working upward. "We ain't always seen eye ter eye along the way. . . ."

He would have gone on, but a call from Tonkawa stopped him. "I could use a hand here!"

Parker swallowed and started to rise, but O'Hearne pushed him down. "You go down the creek a ways with Louie and wash yer ears. I'll come git ya when the job's done."

Louie O'Hearne walked out of sight of the dugout with them. He whistled until Parker asked him, "Did Jesse ever talk about a gal named Lily Bass?"

"He surely did. He said there wasn' no other pullet to hold a candle to her in the whole state a Texas. Did you see her, too?"

"Yep. We both did. She's purty all right. She cried some about Jesse's gettin' killed."

"Tell us what you know about him, Mr. O'Hearne," said Nate.

Louie O'Hearne talked of Jesse and Starr for a time. Then he asked Nate, "Was Jesse kin to ya, too?"

"No," confessed Nate. "I don't have a brother or anybody else. I'm what Parker calls a real leppie. But I sort of feel like I've got somebody now since I've been travelin' with Parker."

Parker looked over at Graber. Nate was as red around the ears as he'd been a little while back. "Who'd that be?"

"All you Quineys, Parker. I suspect you treat me just as badly as you'd treat any real brother."

Parker bit his lip, embarrassed, while Louie O'Hearne laughed at him. Parker looked at his toes and admitted, "Graber, comin' up here I found out ya was a good man some a the time, but that don' say yer gonna be a good one goin' back down home."

A long floating call reached Parker. He took in a big breath of air and started back with Louie and Nate and J.E.B. Stuart. That gun was even heavier now against his hip. Every step a man took wearin' a hogleg reminded him he had one!

Jesse's saddle and other gear were in the wagon. The buryin' box was on the ground beside it, and Amadeo Díaz and Mr. O'Hearne were waiting beside the open tail gate.

Suddenly Parker asked Tonkawa, who stood by with the shovel, "Open it up, Tonkawa."

"Aw right. He's all wrapped up." The old man gave the shovel to O'Hearne, bent down, and pulled off the coffin lid.

Parker went up to the coffin alone. He looked down at the shrouded body, then quickly he unbuckled the gun belt and dropped it and the gun into the box next to the body. Nobody said a word as the Tonkawa Kid slid the lid back on.

Parker was grateful they hadn't. To Tonkawa he said, "Much obliged to ya." He said the same thing to the O'Hearnes and Díaz. Then he got up onto the wagon seat with Nate. There was some daylight left. From now on danged if he was goin' to waste any more of it than he had to. The faster he got home with that buryin' box now the better!

"Are you two colts going back down to Santa Rosa County all alone?" asked Mr. O'Hearne.

"No," said Nate, "the Tonkawa Kid is coming with us."

Tonkawa stood up very straight and said, "Right gladly. That oughta be a good deed, sure enough. I think I knows what's on yer minds right now, but don' never be scared of nobody who's dead, colts. It's the livin' ones ya gotta be afeard of!"

"Amen to that!" came from Mr. O'Hearne, as Tonkawa went to his horse and Parker brought the team around and headed the horses south.

Nate asked Parker, "Will you be scared now that Mr. Bailey's coming with us?"

"Oh, I don' reckon my own brother'd want to haunt me," mumbled Parker. "But now somebody else can go see the Widow Culbertson in Merrick an' tell her the fight wasn't over Lily Bass. I promised her. Tonkawa can do that fer me. She'll be so glad ter hear it, she'll give him some whiskey for certain."

"We could give him one of the bottles of Seminole Elixir, Parker."

Parker said, "Nope, I don' wanta risk that. There's still no tellin' how things'll go with him before we git home. Don' ya forget. He comes from McMullen County, and that's bad man's country."

At that moment Tonkawa trotted up beside them on

201

his wheezing old horse. "Where we headed now?"

"South of the Brazos to a ranch," Nate sang out happily. "I've got to get a letter there to take to a judge in Cottonwood."

"A judge?" The old man looked alarmed.

"It's a letter to help me get out of the clutches of a widow, Mr. Bailey."

The Tonkawa Kid's face took on deep mournful lines. "I'd like nothin' better than gettin' into the clutches of a widder lady, a rich one who's a good looker. I want a lovin' widder who'll call me 'Sweet William' the way my maw used ter."

"Holy Gatlins!" Parker heard Nate exclaim under his breath, making him grin. Yep, that was about the only thing a man could say after hearin' something like that.

10
The
Promises

Riding away from the wagon halfway back to the Brazos, Tonkawa found Comanche "sign," unshod hoofprints near a dead campfire. He was worried when he brought the news to the boys.

"There's Injuns aroun'. We better keep our eyes peeled."

"Oh, don't worry about the Comanches, Mr. Bailey," Nate told him. "We aren't in any danger at all."

This comment made the old man squint. "We ain't? You sure, Nate?"

"Injuns purely hate the sight a Graber here. Havin'

him beside me on the wagon seat's better'n a whole troop of U. S. Cavalry," said Parker.

"Ya don' say?" Tonkawa looked puzzled as he guided his horse to keep pace with the wagon.

"They think I'm a ghost, Mr. Bailey," explained Nate. And then he told the old man about Breaks Lances—exactly as Parker had told the story to him.

To Parker's surprise the Tonkawa Kid didn't laugh. He said after some thought, "Well, I dunno 'bout that, colts. I can't say as I git on with Comanches, them hatin' Tonkawa Injuns, but I don' think it was nice a ya to scare the daylights outa 'em neither."

"But we didn't do it on purpose," protested Nate.

"All the same it got done, didn' it?" Tonkawa touched his chest. "I was in that jailhouse for twenty year. I reckon I oughter know how a body cooped up on a reservation feels. If I'd been this here Breaks Lances, I'd a busted out, too." He looked hopefully and very suddenly into Parker's face. "Ya got some more a that medicine ya gave Nate, boy?"

Parker decided that lying was the best policy. "Naw, when I saw what it done ta Nate, I got rid a it."

While he muttered, Tonkawa kicked his horse into a trot and started down a gully the team would have to skirt. J.E.B. Stuart, his tail frisking, followed him over the rim.

"You lied!" Nate accused Parker.

"You bet I did. Ya watch what else I'm gonna do." Giving the reins to Nate, Parker climbed into the

The Promises

wagon back, opened a sack of supplies, and hauled out the remaining bottles of elixir. He stood up to survey the horizon. Yep, Tonkawa wasn' in sight, and there were some big rocks up ahead. As Nate drove by them, Parker threw the bottles, one by one, against them, smashing the glass. Grinning, he got back onto the seat, but let Nate keep the reins.

"Ya know, Graber, somethin's been puzzlin' me all along."

"What's that?"

"How come all them Hunnicutt folks was up so early the mornin' we chased my dog outa town. It musta been the elixir—the gunpowder in it. I reckon they never did go ter bed the night before!"

Fording the dryin'-up Brazos was easier this time. The Tonkawa Kid had crossed "a hunderd rivers in flood" he'd told them before he reached it, and he proved he knew how by plunging his horse in, showing the team what was expected of them. They followed. Parker was disturbed at getting the coffin wet, but it couldn't be helped. After all, when the sun was hot enough to blister a horned toad under a rock, it would dry out fast.

The Parringtons were glad to see them and asked them to supper as the boys had hoped they would. Sitting next to Tonkawa, who'd copied every knife, fork, and spoon move from Mrs. Parrington at supper, Parker learned that Nate was sure the top man on the

205

Parringtons' string for a fact. He went on jawing about books all the time they were eating, and when Parker tried to get a word in edgewise about the Comanches, Nate gave him the meanest look he'd ever seen on anything but a mule's face.

Later Nate hissed in his ear, "Don't you dare go telling them I got drunk!"

"Why not? They'll want ter know we met Breaks Lances."

"Because they won't want me to come back and live with them if they think I'm drinking. If you bring it up again, I'll do something you won't like one bit. I'll tell them you're an illiterate."

"What's that?"

"Somebody who can't read—that's what!"

Parker chewed this threat over. No, he'd just as soon they didn't know that.

When Nate sat on the sofa with the pretty pullet, Parker kept his eyes on his boots, sulking. Being polite was a strain. He hoped Mr. Parrington wasn't going to read about any more Greeks and hogs.

Suddenly Mrs. Parrington spoke up from her crocheting, "Parker, are you going to write Bonnie Annie Laurie when you get back home? We do get letters here, you know. Riders bring them out from Crawford."

Parker fidgeted, not knowing what to say. He looked helplessly at Nate, who was studying the warts on his thumb like he'd never seen 'em before. "Uh-huh. Sure," he said finally. Nerissa could write for him. She could say he'd busted both a his arms breakin' a horse.

Nate looked up. His lips formed a soundless word Parker would just as soon not know.

Mrs. Parrington fixed up a big feed for them in a cloth and handed it up to Nate as they left the ranch. "God bless you all," she told them, then stood waving with her husband and daughter as they started south. Parker had hoped he'd get another kiss from the heifer calf, but with her ma lookin' on, there wasn' any. But then Graber hadn' got one either, and there was still "P" and "Q" on the back-East tree. The little gal hadn' cut it outa the heart yet.

Parker was silent until late afternoon, though Nate had hummed and whistled all day long. Tonkawa had ridden beside the wagon off and on, but then he swung into it while Nate got down to collect the tuckered-out-looking J.E.B. Stuart.

"Quiney," said the old man, "it appeared to me las' night you and Nate both got eyes fer that little yellow-headed pullet."

"No, I ain't. Her folks are plumb *loco!*"

"No, they ain't. They're nice folks. Wheat's as important as cows and hosses—leastwise, it oughta be someday in Texas. Are ya gonna write her letters? I seen ya was sweet on her."

"I don' see why I should." Parker shot the Tonkawa Kid a you-mind-your-own-business glance. "With old Graber living there, she won' recollect me fer long."

" 'Absence makes the heart grow fonder,' " recited Tonkawa.

" 'Outa sight—outa mind,' " mumbled Parker.

"Ya won' be outa mind if ya write her."

Parker watched Nate chasing J.E.B. Stuart, who'd spotted a prairie-dog town and would rather do some digging than riding in the wagon. He said sharply, "Listen, Tonkawa, I can't write anymore'n you can."

"Do tell!" The old man grinned. "So mebbe ya'll wind up shootin' them round things outa saloon signs, too?"

"No, I won't!" flared Parker. "I ain't gonna be so handy with guns as you was—jes' with horses."

"Well, I didn' think ya was gettin' that savvy." Tonkawa put his hand to his mouth and spoke behind it as if he told a secret. "Did ya ever think with Graber livin' in the same house she is, that heifer'll git the idea he's her brother. That'd give ya the edge on her string."

Parker mused over this. It was *him*—not Nate she'd wanted to be carved on the tree with. Sometimes the Tonkawa Kid made some cow sense after all. Parker gazed toward Nate, who had his dog corralled at last. "I reckon it would," he admitted.

"There ain't nothin' nobody likes more'n in the world than gittin' a letter from a true love. How 'bout me and you learnin' ter read and write?"

"Me and you?"

"Why shouldn' I? Mebbe I got somebody ter write ter, too—mebbe some sheriffs."

Parker shook his head. "I dunno. How're we gonna do that?"

Tonkawa raised a finger and pointed. Nate was coming over the grass to the wagon, lugging a strug- gling J.E.B. Stuart.

"That there's how."

Parker waited until Nate had dumped the dog onto the wagon seat and got up himself. Then as casually as he could, he asked, after Hooraw and Pilgrim had started off again, "You recollect all the times ya wanted ta teach me to read, Nate?"

Nate twisted around, "Sure, I do."

"Well, ya got a willin' pupil—Tonkawa here! He jes' told me he wants ter learn how."

"But what about you, Parker?"

"I reckon I'll listen in. There ain't nothin' else fer me ta do, is there?"

Nate nodded, too happily, Parker thought. To prick his bubble he said, "Ya ain't got no books with ya."

"Oh, I don't need them. I remember the McGuffey primer very well. Stop the team, Parker."

Parker called out "Whoa," and watched Nate leap down and run off to a nearby broomweed bush. In a minute he was back with three stalks. Solemn as two owls, he gave one to Parker, another to Tonkawa, and kept the third for his shirt pocket.

"What's that for?" asked Parker Quiney.

"It's a pen or a pencil. I guess prairie dirt will have to be your slate, though."

Parker looked at the broomweed doubtfully, sighed, and stuck it into his hatband. At least he could learn "B" and "A" and "L" to finish up that heart on the back-East tree someday mebbe.

"Now," said Nate, "we aren't going to waste one minute. Mr. Bailey, I want you and Parker to sing after me, 'A, B, C, D, E, F, G.' "

Parker muttered the letters under his breath. The trip up to Whiskey Creek hadn' been easy, but it appeared to him it'd be lots worse going down home. Thinking of the Parringtons gave him some comfort, though, and wouldn't Nerissa be tickled if he came back readin' and writin'? Mebbe he'd even teach Leo and the weaner gals and Earl, too. If the Tonkawa Kid could learn new tricks, so could Earl.

By twilight Parker was up to "S" in the singsong alphabet Nate taught them and at suppertime up to "Z." After they'd eaten, Tonkawa cleared away some grass to get down to the dirt, and Nate scratched out the letters of the alphabet. When he got into his bedroll, Parker Quiney could name "A" through "M," the letter Nate said he'd recognize again upside down at the tail end of the alphabet.

Graber was a good word chooser to start with, Parker decided later. He taught him and Tonkawa "horse" and "bridle" and "saddle" and "bit" right off. Then he got onto things like "the cat saw the rat," "the cat ate the rat," after he showed them both how

210

to read the letters in cattle brands, something Parker demanded to know first off.

Nate kept up the teaching without resting a minute until they were, as Parker figured it, just one day north of Merrick. When Nate started in on that night's lesson, Parker stopped him. "I got to talk to Tonkawa. You recollect that Lily Bass heifer?"

"Yes, Parker."

Parker called out, "Tonkawa," and the old man came from where he was whittling beside the fire.

"Mr. Bailey, we have a favor to ask of you."

"Any time, Nate. I owe ya plenty fer teachin' me so much."

"It's Parker's favor. He'll tell you about it."

The Tonkawa Kid didn't seem so pleased now, but he listened while Parker explained how he'd promised not to let Lily Bass see him again. "So will ya go find the Widow Culbertson tomorrer and take her the message that Lily didn' have nothin' ter do with them killin' each other."

"Aw right. I'll go because it's a good thing, Quiney. I reckon they's some good in ya after all. Where'm I gonna find this here widder?"

"At the saloon," explained Nate. "You know—the word with the two 'Os' in it."

Tonkawa looked mighty pleased to hear that, but his toothless smile soon faded. "I ain't got no money."

"The widow owns the saloon. She'll stake ya," Parker told him.

"Well, there's widders and widders," complained the old man.

"Don't worry. She'll bust, she'll be so glad ter hear what ya got ter say," promised Parker.

The next afternoon they stopped early when a passing rider told them Merrick was only three miles away. Tonkawa left them camped there, but not before sprucing himself up, currying his hair and his horse with the same comb and washing his face and hands. Parker heard him humming, "Just Before the Battle, Mother," as he rode off. He guessed the old man sure didn't care about the Civil War. That was a Yankee song.

"Think he'll bring any *sopaipilla* bread?" asked Nate.

"It's my horseback opinion, Nate, there ain't no tellin' what he'll do," said Parker. "Well, let's git on with it. Ya want me ter sing them ABC's agin or tell ya some more about that there 'cat' and 'rat' ya like so much?"

At full dark when Tonkawa hadn't returned, Nate called a halt to the lesson. He got up from the fireside and looked toward Merrick. "It seems to me he oughta be back by now, Parker."

"The widow's givin' him somethin' ter wet his whistle on. He'll be along." Parker glanced over at the wagon, black on the prairie, and moved closer to the fire, shivering. He wasn't one bit sleepy.

Half of the summer stars Parker recognized had set when he heard J.E.B. Stuart's growl, then hoofbeats.

The Promises

The boy grabbed at the Winchester near him and brought it up, but before he could call out a challenge he heard the wavering cry, "It's me, colts. Don' shoot."

"Come on in, Tonkawa," shouted Parker, as Nate threw more chips and some twigs onto the fire.

Tonkawa came prancing into the bright glow. Both boys gaped, and Parker let the rifle fall onto his toe. The old gray horse was gone, but it was still the Tonkawa Kid all right—even if his mount was a fiery black. The horse and the old man glistened with bright metal. There was silver all over the saddle and bridle, silver conchas for the hatband of a new white hat, silver on the handle and holster of his gun and silver dangling from his vest. Silver-mounted supporters held up his new purple shirt above the elbows.

"Holy Gatlins!" murmured Nate.

Dumbfounded, Parker asked, "How did you come by that outfit?"

"In a poker game at the widder woman's saloon. I had me quite a time cuttin' my wolf loose. That there's a twenty-dollar bridle and a sixty-dollar saddle." The old man chuckled and snapped one of the sleeve supporters. "This here ain't what ya think it is. That widder woman and me have got us a understandin'. She give these to me. They're her garters. After I get you colts down to Santa Rosa County with that box, I'm ridin' back up here and marryin' up with her." He sat down beside the fire, grinning with happiness. "Did I ever tell ya about the other time I went gallin' and got drunk and it took five men to git me to the jail-house?"

Parker's surprise at the old man's appearance gave way to anger. "Never mind about that, Tonkawa. Did ya give her my message?"

"I sure did, boy. An' she was glad ter hear it." The Tonkawa Kid pulled at his chin as if trying to remember. Then he chuckled and went on. "She wanted ter know if ya was still the brass monkey she thought ya was, and I said you was improvin' a little bit because a the good work Nate and me was doin' on ya. She said ter tell ya she hoped ya'd never mess around with guns like yer brother. I told her what you done with yer brother's hogleg. She said she didn' reckon no Quiney'd ever have that much sense."

Parker looked at Tonkawa's glittering silver splendor, ignoring the insults. "Yer sure fast at courtin' widows, ain't ya, Tonkawa?"

"I gotta be. I ain't got so much time anymore," said the old man, pushing the coffeepot into the coals. "I keep forgettin', though. The widder woman said to give ya this." Parker watched the old man get up and go to some new saddlebags, unbuckle them, and haul out something wrapped in a big checkered napkin. "She recollected you leppies was mighty partial to the Mexican bread her cook fries up."

"Thank you, Mr. Bailey," said Nate, grinning.

With the checkered cloth tied over J.E.B. Stuart's

mouth to keep him from barking and Nate holding fast
to his legs on the wagon seat, Parker went through
Hunnicutt after dark. He and Nate had decided that it
wouldn' do for anybody with a good memory to spot
the "mad dog" walkin' around loose. They didn't let
J.E.B. free until they were some miles beyond the
sleeping town.

"Wouldn't you like to know where Professor Tyree
and Madame Maria are?" Nate asked Parker out of
the cool darkness over musical sounds of hundreds of
frogs.

"Not me. They've moved on, I bet. But if I ever run
across them two down home, I'll tell the sheriff what's
in the elixir and how she's a faker. And I'll hold on
ter old El Pollo fer the stew pot."

Nate laughed. "Are we going through Lockville by
night, too, Parker?"

"Naw. I ain't gonna be buff'loed by hell-roarer
Symonds and that blacksmith wife a his—not so close
to Santa Rosa County."

Nate said slowly, "Maybe they're still looking for
us, Parker."

"Mebbe so, but the sheriff'll recollect you and me.
Now you ask me ta spell some words bigger'n 'cat' or
'rat,' huh?"

In spite of his bold words Parker Quiney was scared
when he came into Lockville in broad daylight. But
everything went along like love and kisses until they
reached the middle of the town. At that moment bad

luck brought the gospel shark out onto the porch of the Union House to pick his teeth. He saw the boys, put away the toothpick, pointed, and bellowed, "You get on over here, you limbs of Satan, you orphans of the storm!"

Parker got ready to whip up the team. He guessed he'd better make tracks before Symonds fetched Adelina. "Hang on, Nate," he warned.

But Tonkawa grabbed the reins and stopped him. "I'll tend to it, Quiney, fer ya." Bold as could be he took the black up to the saloon with half of the town gawking at all the silver he was sportin' and his white hat and purple shirt. "Pardon me, sir," Parker heard him say to the preacher. "Was ya addressin' my grandsons, Jonathan an' Parker?"

"I told Tonkawa while you were sleeping the other night all about the Symondses," explained Nate to Parker.

The gospel shark let out a roar. "They're house burners, child arsonists! They're named Ulysses and Sam Houston."

"I oughta know my own lovable lads, shouldn' I? Ya got the wrong boys in mind," said the Tonkawa Kid. "It appears to me ya don' like boys. So'll be sayin' *adiós* ta ya an' this pore little old town!"

Leaving the gospel shark staring after him, speechless, Tonkawa rode back to the wagon. "Git on with it, sonny," he ordered Parker, who started the team out trotting south.

216

"Much obliged to ya, Tonkawa," said Parker three miles out of town.

"Thank you, Mr. Bailey. You were wonderful," added Nate.

"Don' mention it. I wish ya was my grandsons sometimes—even ya, Quiney, 'cause yer improvin' some."

From Lockville to the north bank of the Colorado River took only a few days' traveling. Parker went to the same ford and found the stream low enough to cross without trouble. He halted there, waiting for Tonkawa to take the black across, but the old man had reined in.

"Ain't ya coming?" called Parker to him.

"Nope. Ya said we'd hit town purty soon after we crossed this here river. I think mebbe I recollect Cottonwood, colt. There's no cause fer me to go inter it and some cause ter stay out of it."

"You're wanted there, Mr. Bailey?" asked Nate.

"Well, mebbe so. Is there a little yellow-brick bank there?"

"There sure is," said Parker, "an' there's a little yellow-brick jailhouse, too."

"I reckoned that would be so," mourned the old man. Then he perked up some. "Well, I can't rightly say as how I want ta meet this here Widder Bybee a yers, Nate, and I think one Quiney's enough fer a lifetime fer me."

He grinned at Nate. "Good luck to ya, wisdom

bringer. Thanks fer what ya tried ta teach me. I can read 'cat' now anytime I see it." He took Nate's hand and pumped it, then rode around to Parker's side of the wagon. "*Adiós,* Quiney. I got a few words fer ya first, though."

"What'd they be?" Parker waited warily. You never could tell what this old man was going to say or do.

"Don' never forgit what ya did with that gun a yer brother's. Go raise hosses instead a dyin' young like him. And ya write that little yeller-headed gal up on the Brazos reg'lar, and she won' fergit ya."

"That all, Tonkawa?"

"Almos'."

"Well, what's the rest of it?"

"I wanta hear ya promise Nate an' me ya'll go ter school now—real school here in this town!"

Parker exploded. "That ain't no fair thing ta ask! I did'n make no bargain with ya."

He looked from eye to eye. Tonkawa was looking sternly at him. Nate was looking sterner. Parker Quiney said, scowling. "Aw right, but jes' remember, yer makin' me do it."

The old man slapped his thigh. "That'll make that Nerissa woman ya don' like smile. Calico—females— that's all what makes Texas men be menfolks instead of hogs. Give calico credit fer it. Butter that there Nerissa up, and don' play no poker never."

"That all, Tonkawa?" asked Parker hopefully.

"Jes' about. The las' thing I wanta say afore I go is

218

that ya two colts appear to me ter be cut outa the same bolt a cloth—and full a the same vinegar. I reckon ya knows it by now, don't ya? Well, back ta the arms a the widder in Merrick."

The Tonkawa Kid turned his horse around, took off his gorgeous hat, and waved it. Before he could get his black into a gallop, though, Nate stood up in the wagon and called to him over the brown grass of summer, "Mr. Bailey, remember saloon is spelled s-a-l-o-o-n!"

Neither Parker nor Nate spoke until the team was across the Colorado and they were in Santa Rosa County. Then Parker cleared his throat, and said, "Graber, I think I'm mebbe gonna miss ya."

"Me, too, Parker," said Nate, shaking his hand.

"Are ya goin' ter need help with the Widow Bybee?" asked Parker a few moments later.

"I'm not worried. I'm going right to the judge's office. He likes me. He'll let me live in the jail until I go north. Nobody's going to call me 'despicable biped' anymore and not be sorry. I learned that from you, Parker. You did some teaching, too."

Parker blushed with pleasure, then said, "Nate, if ya need a horse to go up to the Brazos, I'll have Earl sell ya a good one dirt-cheap. Us Quineys owe ya that —fer a lotta things."

Nate nodded. "I'm worried about you, though. It's a couple of months until school starts. I may be gone by then. Did you really mean your promise?"

"I did." Parker shifted unhappily on the wagon seat. "I don' cotton to the idea, mind ya, but if I'm gonna write letters I gotta be able to write 'bout things more'n 'cat' an' 'rat,' don' I? I promised ya and Tonkawa I'll go in spite a my honest opposition."

Nate prompted, "Are you still going to be a bronc snapper?"

This question make Parker scowl. "I ain't so sure I'm not and not so sure I am. Mebbe I'll write ya about it when I make up my mind. Don' ya ride me too hard. I'm only yer second pupil, wisdom bringer. Save yer strength fer some others. Ya got yer way quite a bit lately, it appears ter me. Ya don' have ter go after me like ya was killin' snakes all the time!"

"All right, Parker." And then Nate laughed.

On the outskirts of Cottonwood he suddenly said, "Let me down here, Parker." Nate took his bedding from the wagon, jumped down with it over his shoulder, then reached up to pat J.E.B. Stuart on the wagon seat once more and get his face licked all the way across.

"Good-bye, Parker, until next time. Remember your promise—even if you learn the wisdom bringer here's mean enough to kick even you barefoot—which she is."

Parker looked at Nate's upturned face. Nate wasn't pale anymore. His hair was short curls all over instead of long ones. That was the big improvement. But other than that he hadn't changed. He was as fat as ever.

"Graber," said Parker, "yer a mighty good man to ride a river with!" He stuck out his hand.

"Much obliged, Parker Quiney. So are you." Nate's grin split his face from ear to ear as he shook Parker's hand.

Near sunset Pilgrim and Hooraw pulled up under the big pecan tree close by the Quiney house. When Parker called out, "I'm home," over J.E.B. Stuart's wild barking, Earl and Nerissa and the others came running from all directions like the chickens bein' fed.

"You brought Jesse back, Parker?" asked Earl.

"I done it, Earl."

Earl told him, "You done good, Parker, I'm proud a ya, boy."

"It wasn' so much. I can't take so much pride in it." Parker ducked his head toward his sister-in-law and removed his hat. "Havin' a lot a pride's a sin," he said direct to her. He was pleased at the sudden "welcome home" smile she gave him.

Then he looked down at the smallest weaner gal, who'd stuck her arm inside the wheel spokes like she always did when she was near the wagon. He'd have to hold the team steady or she'd bust it again like the las' time she done that fool thing.

"You and J.E.B. been gone a while, Parker," she said.

"I reckon I have, honey. It's a long way to Whiskey Creek!"

221

Author's Note

For several years now teachers, school administrators, and librarians have asked me to write a "book for boys." *A Long Way to Whiskey Creek* is the result of a good deal of preliminary thinking, though. It's always been my contention that little grips the imagination and holds the interest of most people quite as much as the Old West. And from observing boys (and girls) I believe that nothing intrigues them more than "being on the move." Hence, I combined the two for this book.

Although I traveled to Texas going over the territory Parker, Nate, and J.E.B. Stuart supposedly covered nearly a century ago, I have used fictional names for most of the towns they stopped in—Cottonwood, Merrick, Hunnicutt, and Ruination. I have set them in real countryside, however, and Buffalo Notch is the actual semi ghost town of Buffalo Gap, outside Abilene, Texas. The rivers, the Colorado and Brazos, are very real "rivers to cross."

The trail herd details are as accurate as I could make them without having participated in a real stampede. The Comanche lore is factual. They were a remarkable tribe. It is true that a renegade band left the reservation in 1879 and wandered in north Texas. My chief source on these Indians was *The Comanches, Lords of the South Plains* by Ernest Wallace and E. Adamson Hoebel.

I've tried to give the flavor of Texas speech in the late nineteenth century without being too technical for today's non-horse-or-cow-oriented reader. To find these examples of "Texas talk" I've read quite a few writings of nineteenth-century cowboys and "characters." Very useful were *The Log of a Cowboy* by Andy Adams, *Mean as Hell* by Dee Harkey, *The Old-Time Cowhand* by Ramon F. Adams, and the *Cowboy Reader,* edited by Lon Tinkle and A. Maxwell.

I found looking at the paintings of Frederic Remington and Charlie Russell helpful for costume details. Two articles, in particular proved to be very important—one written by a bewildered transplanted Scot in Texas, in 1876, and the other by an Abilene schoolboy. They are "The Cow Walks Neatly; Texas in 1876" by William Alexander Bowie, *Southwest Review,* Winter 1959, and *Buffalo Gap, the Living Ghost Town* by Michael Bonine in *The Junior Historian,* September 1959.

Many librarians aided my research. The staffs of the University of California, Riverside Library and of the Riverside Public Library deserve their usual credit.

People who were specifically of help were Miss Thelma Andrews, of the Abilene Public Library, who sent much material on the Buffalo Gap area, and Mr. L. Tuffly Ellis, Assistant Director of the Texas State Historical Association, who confirmed by documenta-

223

tion my thesis that there was Union sentiment in Texas during the Civil War. I wish also to thank Mrs. Ross Hendrick, of Vernon, Texas, for her help and Miss Laurie Dudley, Children's Coordinator at the Dallas Public Library, for her interest and enthusiasm. My husband and daughter and I should also convey our gratitude to Edward and Polly McCormick, of Abilene, who showed us old Buffalo Gap, Texas, when the grass was green and the bluebonnets in bloom.

My teen-age daughter, Ann, must also be commended for naming a good many of the characters in this book and for dreaming up the escape sequence at the end of Chapter 3 when I was stuck for a way for Parker and Nate to leave Hunnicutt in a hurry.

Patricia Beatty
December, 1969